Stella's Scream

AN EXTREME HORROR NOVELLA

First Printing in 2026

Publisher: Julie Hiner

KillersAndDemons.com

Editing by: Taija Morgan

Cover Design: Fabled Beast Design | A. A. Medina

ISBN: 978-1-7389176-4-8

First Edition

Trigger Warnings

This is a work of extreme horror. The story includes topics of extreme violence, murder, torture, mutilation, sex, masochism, and rape. Stella's journey is not for everyone. Please consider this before following her into a pool of blood.

Dedication

To Stella.

Your voice screamed from the depths of my soul.

Contents

Playlist   1

Sanity   3

1. Post Slaughter   5

2. Postcard   9

3. Bum Steer   12

4. Filthy Fuck   17

5. Rusty Nail   20

6. Heavy Metal and Wrestling   23

7. Nü-Metal Purge   28

8. Homicidal Ideation   36

Innocence   39

9. Hot and Bothered   41

10. Terrorizer   47

11. Red Room   50

12. Carnal Cougar   53

13. Killing Time   61

14. Creature Corpse   64

15. Chicken Coop   68

16. Brad's Bytes   71

17. Wasteland   78

18. Laboratory Lunatic   81

19. Fish-Child   85

20. Innocence   91

21. Slice and Sew   94

22. Release Me   101

23. Too Pure for a Purge   106

Love   109

24. Atomic Liquor   111

25. Henricas   114

26. Sacrifice   118

27. Dismembered Dorah   123

28. Thirteenth Angel   126

29. Stella's Scream   130

30. Pavilion   133

31. Rust   136

About Author   141

Acknowledgments   143

Also By   145

Playlist

PHONEY SMILES & FAKE HELLOS
STRONGER THAN DEATH
SUPERTERRORIZER
JUST KILLING TIME
PEDDLERS OF DEATH
13 YEARS OF GRIEF
ALL FOR YOU
LOVE REIGN DOWN
RUST

SANITY

Chapter 1
Post Slaughter

Trails of sticky blood snaked over her fingers and down her arms. Splattered shapes covered her face like a deformed Rorschach collage. Images of ichor-soaked flesh flashed through her mind. The last twenty-four hours of Stella's life played on repeat.

It wasn't the first time she'd sliced her human prey wide open and watched their innards spill out and slop over the ground, spraying copper zested droplets across her lips. The lust and exhilaration coursing through her veins was a clear sign it wouldn't be the last.

She uncurled her fingers from her death grip on the steering wheel and reached over to crank the volume on the cassette deck. A manic beat blasted through every inch of space in the Chevrolet Chevelle. A guttural guitar riff ripped from the speakers, alternating with primal squeals. Barbaric vocals accused Stella of indulging in a power trip. *Black Label Society's* newest album. *Stronger Than Death.* The title reflected exactly her emotional state. The track, "Phoney Smiles & Fake Hellos", showcased Zakk Wylde's signature sound at the most untamed and raw she'd ever heard.

It had been nearly two years since she'd sliced the eighteen-year-old serial killer, known as the Torture Queen, from neck to anus. With her own medieval torture axe. In her own dungeon. Using her own techniques on her youthful flesh. The moment Stella drew blood, she destroyed the life she had striven for. Something snapped within.

Following a long, lonely road of stalking, hunting, and killing, there was no end in sight. Stella wasn't slowing down. Kill after kill, the desire to hunt again continued to burn in her gut.

But this time...this last kill was *different.*

That motherfucker wasn't human. The Red River Ripper. Hiding in a shack full of bodies, a few miles off the deserted road of the River of No Return. He was a monster. He deserved to die. If she hadn't gutted him and left him to bleed out, no one would have stopped him. So sick of watching psycho deranged killers slip through the loose grip of the law, she wouldn't let these fuckers reign the earth any longer. She couldn't. At twenty-four-years old, she replaced her rookie detective badge with a hunting knife fit for a beast.

With plenty of gore on her hands, and aching for something more, her new path opened up wide in front of her the moment she busted the Red River Ripper's door open and saw the rotting corpses of six young girls strung up like animal carcasses, swaying back and forth, skin slick with sweat, privates oozing with semen, and heads lolling against their chests.

Something unleashed, awakened deep within her. It was her premier of licking the blood and bodily fluids of her prey dripping from her blade. As the sour liquid trickled down her throat, a feral being stirred within her and clawed its way out.

Hell, it had burst free. Now satisfied for the moment, it crawled inward to wait for the next slaughter.

As she turned the wheel in a sharp right, the tires barely gripping the gravel road, dust clouded in a thin veil between her and the world. She ached for her physical reactions to her savage kill to remain vivid. Her hand still flushed from the heat of the gore gushing from the gaping cut as she pressed the blade deeper into the spongy flesh of her wounded prey. She still felt the resistance of his intestines against the steel as she twisted the handle. His screams of agony continued to ring through her ears, and his cold, piercing stare sent a fresh wave of chills down her back.

Desperation filled her soul. Anger boiled in her veins. She couldn't watch another young, innocent victim die. Sometimes a tiny thought—*what had she become?*—tapped at the back of her mind. Every time she shoved it into a dark crevice.

It was her destiny to purge the world of the monstrous murderers.

She exhaled sharply, her bourbon-laced breath hot against her nostrils, and eased back against the soft pleather headrest. As Zakk's rough voice belted out the last verse, the words of a hardcore rush and not fucking caring nestled into the corners of Stella's mind. She relished the rotten metallic taste of death clinging to her tongue and staining her throat.

The crimson-orange sun simmered over the horizon, welcoming the night, and beckoning her down the open desert road. A fire raged in her loins, desperate for release.

She needed bourbon. And metal. She knew where to find it. The epic vocalist serenading her from the speakers now was starting a tour within a few days' drive from here.

The life of a killer was lonely. Didn't Billy the Kid have a team of sidekicks? Would she ride or die alone, or would she have a partner? There was only one possibility in her mind. A long shot. But worth a crack.

Chapter 2
Postcard

Pressing the pen hard against the card stock until the ink bled into a black pool, she scratched out the *'love'* and left the signature as a cold and simple *'Stella'*. What had gotten into her?

The note she'd scribed was tight. Brief. It made her point.

You'd like it here. Quiet. Open. Peaceful.

At least...I think you would. If I'd gotten to know you...

The anonymity made it possible for her to express a bit of what she really wanted to say. She didn't even address it to its recipient.

Bryce.

His amber eyes and dark hair remained crystal clear in her mind, refusing to leave. She hadn't even said goodbye when she left. The last time she saw him, she'd forced herself on him, begging for him to numb her grief. The heat of his tongue still burned between her legs, and the sweetness of his lips still lingered on hers.

She flipped the postcard over and stared at the tangerine-filtered image of a lonely desert town. It looked like every single one she'd seen over the last thirty-six hours of cruising through the open Nevada desert. It was like the prairies back home…open space with the occasional cookie-cutter town. After a while, you forgot where you were.

The dirty-blonde middle-aged waitress returned, a scowl plastered to her face, telling the world that she was less than impressed with where her life had taken her.

"More?" The server grunted as she lifted a coffee pot and pointed at the empty cup on the table.

"Sure." Stella attempted as big a smile as she could.

As *Dee,* according to the scratched name tag pinned crookedly to the woman's uniform, poured the last drop of burned coffee, she stood back and sighed. "You're far too pretty and young to look so tired, honey." She pressed her knuckles into her waist.

Stella nodded as she ran her fingers through the dark strands of her hair. She missed her strawberry-blonde curls. "Too much to do." She looked up at Dee hovering over her like a caring grandmother.

"I get ya. Want me to post that? I can send it with our outgoing." She tapped the postcard with a perfectly manicured nail.

"Yeah, sure." Stella watched the card slide across the table, wishing she could read the note again, but knowing if she didn't let it go now, she might never send it.

She chugged half the coffee as she dropped a crumpled five-dollar bill on the table. Slipping her arms into her leather jacket, she strode to the door and out into the heat of the desert. Walking toward her car, she flipped her phone open and dialled the number she'd been dying to call for too long.

After a single ring, Iris picked up. "Agent Quesnel."

Stella swallowed. Her voice came out meek. "It's Stella."

Iris responded in her usual sultry tone. "I've been thinking about you. It's been a while."

"Almost two years."

"You vanished after that case...the official statement was that you resigned." Iris said.

"It was time." Stella bit her bottom lip.

"No badge." Sex seeped from Iris' voice.

"I've been..." she held back, rerouted the conversation. "I need an off-the-rails metal-bourbon-sex bender. Preferably one kissed with cherry lips." Sweat trickled down the back of Stella's neck as she rushed the words out before she could change her mind.

Who the fuck did she think she was? Former homicide detective turned killer. The only rules she played by now were her own. During a hunt, she dripped with confidence, knowing she could smell a serial killer from miles away. The sound of Iris' voice turned her into a kitten with a tiny meow. She longed to breathe in the woman's cinnamon scent. To savour her cherry-kissed lips.

Silence hung on the line. Stella clenched her jaw as she waited. Why would a woman like Iris—an FBI agent, for Christ's sake—join her bloody quest? Yet something told her she wasn't crazy for taking a shot. All she'd done was invite the woman for a night of metal. They met for the first time in the lust-filled green room after an epic concert. This wasn't crazy. She wasn't insane.

Iris sighed. "I thought you'd never ask."

Chapter 3
Bum Steer

The wood-panelled walls dripped with several decades of strong booze and perspiration. A multitude of antlers protruded between crookedly hung photos of the plethora of rock and metal bands that had played at the *Bum Steer* over the years. An odour of burned plastic clung to the dank space. The red-and-white-striped, barn-like structure with massive wooden doors had become Tucson's heavy metal belly. Rumbling erupted from the back of the stage. The wild crowd lurched like a group of undead smelling the living.

Sparks ignited in the pit of Stella's belly. She *needed* a shot of metal heroine now more than she ever had before. The moment would be perfect...once she laid eyes on the woman she was here to meet. Grazing her face with her fingertips, Stella moved stray strands of black hair from her face and searched the entire joint again. A nervous ball roiled through her gut. It had been nearly two years. Sparks of lust still ignited in Stella's loins every time she whispered her name...*Iris.*

Fire hair and arctic eyes grasped Stella's attention. She focused on the woman she'd been dying to see, willing her to respond. The woman saw her, and their gazes locked. Two shades of blue—ice and sky, holding a passion-fuelled moment.

Iris walked toward her. FBI agent and criminal profiler, A.K.A. bourbon-drinking, heavy metal addict, whom Stella had first met in a green room at the Warehouse in Toronto, Canada, after a Queensrÿche concert. She could still imagine her own skin sizzling under the touch of Iris' hot tongue. The woman had to be twenty years older than her, yet her smooth ivory skin spoke otherwise.

"Stella." Iris wrapped her arms around her in a tight embrace.

The affection melted Stella. Something she rarely did. But this was unlike any normal situation.

As they pulled away from each other, Stella looked into Iris' eyes again. "You came."

"Honey, the only thing that could keep me away from a call from you is one of my beloved serial killers. At the moment, there seems to be a break in sadistic slayings." She smirked.

"Unusual."

"Yeah. Well...you and I both know it's a facade. Fuckers keep slipping under the radar. Law enforcement protocols need a revamp." Iris toyed with a strand of Stella's hair. "Black. I like it."

"Trying *not* to be found." A pang gripped her heart as she relived the snipping sound of the scissors through her strawberry blonde curls.

A dark stone hanging from a chain around Iris' neck caught Stella's attention. She ran her finger along the smooth gem. "Pretty."

Iris lifted the stone and ran her finger down the sharpened tip, drawing a droplet of blood. "Obsidian. Sharp enough to cut a lot of things. And..." she pressed a tiny silver sphere at the top of the jewel. It unlatched from the chain. "It's come in handy a couple of times when I found myself in a bind." She latched it back onto the chain.

"Impressive." Stella smirked.

Iris shot a glance at the bar along the side wall. "We need a drink."

Without hesitation, Stella followed Iris, scanning the rows of glass bottles along the top shelf, hoping for Maker's Mark. A guitar riff blasted an electric shot through the entire space. The crowd erupted in a group roar.

"Double bourbon. Two," Iris yelled over the noise at the pale, skinny server behind the bar.

Stella leaned in close to Iris, breathing in her cinnamon scent. "You ever seen him before?"

"Mr. Wylde?"

Stella nodded.

"Nope. Heard he performs like a real legend." Iris took the drinks and handed one to Stella. "I can't believe he's playing *here*."

"I saw an interview. He came off Ozzfest a couple of months ago. Black Label Society tour starts tomorrow. Here in Tucson. Convention Center." Stella relished a long sip of her double bourbon.

"Tomorrow?"

"Yeah. Says he loves the intimate performances, and playing the night before a big stadium tour keeps him connected to his music and his fans."

Iris licked her top lip. "Mmm...you'd *love* to be connected with him...wouldn't you?"

Stella practically snorted. "No shit." To be honest, the thought of it made every part of her body flush. She'd devoured plenty of metal and rock stars, eating them up and walking away without an ounce of attachment. Zakk's mountain man physique and his metal angel voice pulled her in hard. She doubted one round with him would be enough.

"This will be epic. But...you called me here for more than a night of bourbon and metal," Iris stated. It wasn't a question.

"Maybe." Stella sipped her drink seductively.

Iris hovered at the back of the crowd. "What did you have in mind?"

"Like you said...law enforcement protocols need a re-haul. Hell, I'm tired of rules. I'm sick of psychotic killers getting away with murder." She took a deep breath. "I'm on the hunt."

Iris nodded. "And you're looking for a partner?"

"I know it's a long shot..."

Iris pressed her fingertip against Stella's lips. "Maybe not. Let's blow off some steam...then we'll talk."

A guitar squeal and a bass beat grabbed their attention. The drummer, bassist, and secondary guitarist were now positioned, warming up the fans. The restless crowd packed tight up front, lunging at the tiny stage. Iris slipped her hand into Stella's and guided her through the mob like she owned the place. As they approached the front, the barely elevated stage taunting them, the ultimate guitar chord vibrated through the air, reaching Stella's heart. It was him. The metal man that she'd been dying to see for a long time.

The first few chords of "Stronger Than Death", the signature song from the album with the same name, vibrated through the entire space. She closed her eyes and let the deep, guttural sound, like something from the depths of hell, seep through her pores and slither through her veins. The singer's rough voice gripped her soul, telling her to look inside, to find herself, that bones would break and blood would be lost.

Chapter 4
Filthy Fuck

Stella's cheek pressed against the cold, sticky tiles of the bathroom stall. Soft, moist lips pressed up against the plumpest portion of her ass. A shiver ran up her spine as Iris guided her tongue along Stella's rump flesh, underneath the crook of her ass, and down to the sweetest part of her. Stella slid her face up along the wall and rolled her eyes back. The urine-tinged air trickled up her nostrils. She breathed it in. She wanted this. *Needed* this. A filthy fuck in the human liquid-coated bathroom of a dank metal joint.

It was the only way she could achieve sexual release. Without release, she would likely implode. After an utterly satisfying two-hour set by Mr. Wylde, Stella was on fire. Everything about the night had been dead-on. Almost.

The only thing *off* was that the woman performing lip service on her wasn't a stranger. Resisting Iris was impossible.

As Iris slid her tongue further into Stella's sweet spot, hot tingles erupted up her body. Her shoulders shook. Her body shuddered. The eruption reached deep inside her.

Without hesitation, Stella spun around and ran her hands up Iris' arms, then wrapped her fingers around the woman's supple breasts. She pushed Iris back against the wall, then crouched down, planting lingering kisses along Iris' body. As she approached the forbidden, fiery lust sizzled deep down. She pulled Iris' leather pants down over her curvaceous hips, then licked her inner thigh. Her skin tasted of cherry whiskey. Saliva pooled at the back of Stella's throat. She dared to look up at Iris. Iris stared back, her ice-blue eyes hypnotizing her.

Breathing in the sweet scent of this intoxicating woman, Stella ran her fingers over the red lace keeping her goods *off limits.* Iris tilted her head back, her fire hair spreading over the tiled wall. A strand caught on a glob of pink bubble gum wedged in a crack.

Pulling the lace over the creamy flesh of Iris' thighs, Stella slid her tongue between Iris' soft, pink lips. Iris moaned. Heat shot through Stella. She closed her eyes and worked her way deep into Iris, tasting the whiskey cherry flavour dripping from her juices.

Stella swallowed back the sweet liquid. Iris ground her ass into the wall. Pushing her face into Iris, Stella swirled her tongue. Moans of pleasure erupted through the small stall. Iris' legs quivered, then her body went limp.

Stella stood, pulled the lace and leather back over Iris' curves, then slithered her way up to meet Iris with a hard kiss.

As they parted, their eyes locked.

Iris, still breathless, whispered between pants, "Shall we?"

Stella nodded, then clicked open the rusty lock on the stall door.

As she walked through the bathroom, shimmering with neon orange lights that flickered, fighting to stay alive, she replayed Iris' words through her mind.

"It can only be once."

Did Iris really mean it?

As filthy as it was, there was something *pure* about it. Stella doubted she'd be able to resist the urge to kiss those cherry lips again.

Chapter 5
Rusty Nail

The smoky-sweet bourbon burned Stella's throat. The alcohol numbed the throbbing at the base of her skull, easing what she swore would be a much worse hangover than it was. Her tolerance was at an all-time high, and there was no end in sight.

Despite the fire they started in the bathroom stall at the Bum Steer, they'd slept in separate rooms at the Sunland Motel. Iris swore it was for the best. Stella had lain in bed, staring at the low-hanging stucco ceiling, wondering if it really was. Hell would have to turn to ice before she'd admit it, but Stella suspected she was actually growing tired of being alone.

When they stumbled out of the motel into the heat of the desert town, it was nearly noon. Desperate for a good dose of the hair of the dog, they walked across the street to the Rusty Nail, where the sign out front promised the joint was *here for you* with *friends old and new.*

Iris reached across the table, stroking Stella's hand with soft fingertips and bringing her back to the present moment. "You know it was just the one time. It has to be...if..."

"If we're really doing this," Stella finished Iris' sentence, locking her gaze on the woman's ice-blue eyes. The stare, intense, unlike anything Stella had ever experienced, churned a fire in her belly and sent a hot flush up her arms and down her back.

Iris took a healthy pull of her own bourbon, her cherry lip dipping into the amber liquid. She set the glass down with a click. "Yeah. I'll be your killer, but I can't mix this…" She licked her top lip, "with murder. We need to be focused. We can't fuck up."

Stella sat back against the chair. "I agree." She pushed her emotions down into the pit of her belly. After another pull of her drink, she broached the topic swelling in her mind. "Why? I was hoping…but it seemed a bit of a stretch. I thought the FBI was your life."

Iris sighed. Her nostrils flared. She took a large gulp of her drink. "I'm on probation."

Stella raised an eyebrow. Could it be FBI Agent Quesnel was as ill-behaved as she was?

"Mutilator Mort. What the press called my last case. I've only ever seen something this fucked up once. Young girls. I mean…*young*." She took another drink and closed her eyes. "He earned the world record for mutilation." As she rubbed circles on her temples, she reopened her eyes. They were glistening.

Stella's heart seized. "Let me guess…he was slipping through the fingers of the law."

Iris nodded. "I knew where he'd strike next. The level of detail in the profile I'd built was beyond any I'd ever created." She leaned over the table. "I could *feel* his next move."

"A feeling isn't enough for a secret swat." Stella huffed.

"It's not enough for fucking anything. I went in. Against orders."

Stella explored the lines etching Iris' face. "You got him?"

Iris smirked. "Real good. Gave him a serving of his own signature."

"Good."

"Yeah. But...it's like I blacked out...when things came clear again...Jesus..." She wiped her hands over her face. "There were pieces of him that were unrecognizable...they weren't even part of him anymore."

"I get it. I had similar experiences." Her blade twisting the Red River Ripper's intestines until his internal fluids poured from his body flashed through Stella's mind, vivid and real, reminding her of who she was.

Iris guzzled the rest of her bourbon. "We have to do this. There's no other way."

Stella nodded. She breathed in Iris' sweet scent wafting across the table and shut out any sexual desire for this incredible woman. The woman who was now her slaughter sidekick.

Her gut told her the killing spree they were about to embark on would be a bloodbath like no other.

Chapter 6
Heavy Metal and Wrestling

The engine hummed, Iris and Stella hunched down in the front seats of the black Trans-Am, out of the glow of the streetlights. They'd ditched the pretty green Chevelle before crossing the border into Mexico. With limited security in the rural desert, it had been surprisingly easy to break into Sam's Scrap-A-Lot and perform an after-dark exchange. A warm breeze played with Stella's loose hair; her elbow rested on the ledge of the open window. Fall was reaching into winter, but the heat of the desert clung like a desperate child.

"We should go in. Scope out the place." Iris stared intently across the street at the neon-blue sign.

Lopez Mateos. An arena in *Tlalnepanthla de Bax,* outside of Mexico City, known for heavy metal and wrestling matches.

"Wait till we see someone who fits the profile."

Iris nodded, pressing her head back against the seat. The white-blonde dye they'd applied hid all remnants of the luscious fire red. It was taking some getting used to.

Focusing on the entrance, Stella examined the constant stream of young people holding out their tickets for the thick-muscled bouncer. Baggy jeans, white tank tops and hoodies were in abundance on the bodies of tonight's crowd.

The nü-metal scene was rapidly blossoming. A man old enough to be out of place in the young crowd approached the door. The breeze swept the strands of his black-as-night hair away, exposing a series of piercings up the side of his earlobe.

Stella sat up and leaned in toward the windshield. "It's him."

Iris peered out the passenger-side window, narrowing her eyes. "You sure?"

Obituary, permanently etched in black ink dripping with red on the side of the man's neck, confirmed Stella's suspicions. This was a nü-metal concert. They were looking for someone familiar with death metal lyrics, specifically by *Obituary.*

"Tattoo. On his neck. It's the logo for the death metal band."

"And...this is a *new-age* metal concert?" Uncertainty riddled Iris' statement.

"Nü-metal." Stella smirked.

"Dammit." Heat flushed Iris' face. "I'm out of my league. I *thought* I was a metalhead."

"You are."

Iris grabbed for the door handle.

"Let's wait," Stella said.

"Really?" Iris' knee shook rapidly.

"I know you're eager. Trust me, I'm dying to make this motherfucker bleed. I think that was him. Let's keep our distance. We'll go in once the music starts." Stella touched Iris' arm.

"Watch him choose his victim." Iris clicked the door shut.

"Follow him after. To his killing room." Tingles erupted up Stella's arms.

"Catch him in action." Iris licked her top lip, raising an eyebrow.

Stella nodded. "Gut him where it counts. Leave him surrounded by evidence. When the authorities find him...they won't give a shit. They'll see what a maniac he is."

Iris half snorted, half laughed. "Are all death metal lovers so obvious? I mean...that tattoo...the tips of the letters so sharp and covered in red, like blood...it looks Satanic."

"I don't have a Satanic tattoo." Stella laughed. She wondered if Iris had noticed the fresh ink up the side of her arm.

"True. But he's hardcore. Like you."

"I guess." Stella bit her bottom lip.

"I'm still floored you solved this." The look in Iris' eyes caused hot pricks up Stella's arms.

"Any real metal fan would've pieced this together." To Stella, it was so fucking obvious.

Three bodies. Spread out randomly, or so it seemed. The first one turned up in November of last year in Tampa. Last June, a second one appeared, also in Tampa. The authorities found a third last August in St. Petersburg. The time gap and lack of leads caused the first two cases to go cold. Jurisdictional boundaries prevented a connection with the third one. She'd seen it too many times. Lack of resources. Failure to connect the dots. Those were the excuses. They were probably terrified to touch it, clinging to the hope that the crazed killer had moved on.

Halfway through a thick slice of sweet cherry pie, Stella saw the connection the moment she placed the articles from the *Tampa Tempo,* the *Florida Fabricator,* and the *St. Petersburg*

Print, side by side on the table at the roadside diner. The glaring link between them was the message molded from the flesh in their torsos. These somewhat trashy papers reported the words were simply the ramblings of a madman, nothing but lunatic gibberish.

Three lines, all including the words *rot your soul* or *feed your soul.*

They were lyrics from three different Obituary songs. In November 1988, the death metal band played at the Sunset Club in Tampa. There was a gap in their tour, which they resumed at the A.F.B. Warehouse in Tampa in June 1989, then at Jannus Landing in St. Petersburg in August 1989.

Stella suspected it wasn't a coincidence that three bodies had turned up carved with lyrics from songs of the band that had played within the same months at the same locations. It was over ten years later, and the bands now playing were *nü-metal.* Some music aficionados said that death was dead and nu was in. Stella couldn't disagree more.

It didn't take her long to identify the tour the killer was taking, attending live shows at the same series of venues. After playing at Jannus Landing, Obituary had moved on to New Mexico. If her instincts were right, the killer's next victim would be here tonight, at the arena, taking in a *Pulse Punisher* show.

Hardcore death metal fans had a distaste for the new wave of nü-metal. They didn't like the mixing of other genres, like hip-hop, with their idea of pure metal. If her instincts were right, the killer was a death metal enthusiast making some sort of statement. The *Nü-Metal Killer,* as she'd profiled him, had a genuine passion for metal and a desire for blood. Just like her. He was on a purge. Was she any different from him?

"Death metal profiler. That's what you are." Iris shifted restlessly in her seat.

Profiler. Slayer. Masochist. She wasn't sure what she was anymore. Whatever she had been was long gone. What she was becoming would only become clear in time. Her transformation had only begun. The only thing she was sure of was that her hunger for blood was simmering on high, reaching dangerously close to scathing.

Chapter 7
Nü-Metal Purge

S tella steered the Trans-Am down the deserted road, lights off, barely stepping on the gas pedal. Iris leaned out the rolled down passenger-side window, gazing down to where the Nü-Metal Killer had driven his beat-up pickup truck, leaving peels of rust in his wake. Rows upon rows of abandoned railway crates filled the otherwise empty lot.

Stella pulled over and killed the engine. The last thing she wanted was to alert their prey.

Lurking in the shadows of the perimeter of the arena, they watched him lure a young man out of the arena well before the end of the set. The killer coaxed the young man into his truck, then administered something that knocked him right the fuck out.

From a safe distance, staying undetected, Stella followed the truck out to a green space with gardens and monuments. The Nü-Metal Killer parked beside one of the abandoned crates painted in an offensive shade of green and then pulled the lifeless body out of his truck. He must be far more charming than he appeared. It shocked Stella that one of these young metal fans would befriend a guy ten years older and looking like a creep.

"Let's take it from here on foot," Stella whispered.

Iris nodded. They opened their doors slowly, keeping the creaks to a minimum.

Stella reached into the back seat, grabbed her long sleeved Queensrÿche shirt, and pulled it over her head. As she slid her arms into the sleeves, Iris walked around the hood of the car.

"A token from the night we met?" Iris' silky voice caused an eruption of chills up Stella's arms.

"Yeah." Stella bit her bottom lip as the memory of the heat from Iris' tongue swelled between her thighs. More than a reminder of their fiery first encounter, the shirt had become her warrior attire.

Music suddenly blasted from within the crate. An unearthly howl erupted over a savage baseline. Stella couldn't help but smirk. Iris raised an eyebrow.

"'Bloodsoaked.' By Obituary," Stella stated.

Stella led the way down the deserted road to the end of the chain-link fence surrounding the parking lot. An opening cut crudely into the metal, exposing a square large enough for a small vehicle. As she descended the steep descent over a patch of gravel, she eased her boots into the dirt, not wanting to cause a mini landslide. When her boot clicked against the solid pavement, she wrapped her hand around the walnut wood handle of her Beast Hunter knife, and pulled it from its leather sheath. She followed Iris slowly across the deserted parking lot.

Her heart beat a wild rhythm. Sweat trickled down her spine and pooled in the curve at the base of her back. It was thrilling hunting on her own terms. No rules. No badge to suffocate her instincts. A pure hunt. A pure *kill*. Saliva saturated the back of her tongue and drizzled down her throat. Her hunger for justice was greater than she'd realized. Or was it an addiction to the taste of blood? Was she becoming as psychotic as her prey?

When they reached the door, they halted. A whiff of spice sweetened the air as Iris leaned in close.

A shriek shot from within the crate, even louder than the blasting music. It seemed they had not alerted their prey. It also seemed he was working on his latest victim.

Iris raised her hand and held up three fingers for their countdown.

One…

Two…

Three. They kicked the door with a mighty double-booted force. Metal crunched and shards flew, clinking across the crate floor.

Amid his work, the Nü-Metal Killer jumped, standing up at the head of a silver table. The bold letters of the Obituary logo plastered to his shirt stretched tight against his chest. The victim sprawled out on his back, naked and shivering. Dirt and sweat coated his body in a filthy sheen. An orange glow crawled up the back wall from tall candles positioned in ornate holders. A double arch encased in a circle, the symbol of nü-metal, was painted in red over a canvas plastered to the wall. A large black X criss-crossed over the symbol, as if trying to make it die.

The killer recovered from their startling intrusion and gripped the carving knife in his hand. He pressed the pointed tip of the narrow, straight blade against the young man's throat. His crazed eyes bored into them. The victim whimpered.

"Who the *fuck* are you?" the killer yelled over the savage music.

"Put the knife down." Iris' voice conquered the pounding bass.

The killer held the handle in a white-knuckled grip. A drop of blood burst from the victim's throat. "Don't come a step closer. Or he's a dead man."

Stella inspected the torso of the victim. From the base of his chest to the middle of his abdomen, fresh slices, drizzling with blood, outlined a square. Peeled from the top, the skin curled away from the body, revealing the first raised letters in a forming message.

"He's already a dead man." Stella smirked as she took a step closer.

"Then this won't matter." He hissed. His hand twitched.

Stella threw her Beast Hunter at him with a flick of her wrist. It twirled and spun through the air, making several revolutions before lodging straight into the man's shoulder. His weapon dropped to the ground with a loud clink. He clutched his shoulder, blood pouring over his fingers. He crumpled to the ground.

Stella walked up to her target and stared him in the eyes as she pressed her boot against the handle of her weapon, pushing the blade deeper into the open wound.

He yelled out in pain as he clawed at the air with his blood-crusted fingers.

"Bitch." His voice was a gravelly whisper.

She leaned in toward him and fumed, "You have *no* idea."

He spat a wad of soiled saliva onto her cheek. As it drizzled down her face, her lips stretched into a sadistic grin.

Gripping the handle, she yanked her knife from his flesh with a loud squelch. He yelled like a wild beast.

"He's losing a lot of blood." Iris leaned over the victim.

Taking advantage of Stella's loss of focus, the Nü-Metal Killer grabbed his knife and thrust his body upward. Stella stumbled back. The killer's blade sliced through Stella's Queensrÿche shirt, from the top of her left breast to the outer circle of her nipple. The cut was just deep enough to sting like a motherfucker. Her loins moistened.

She lunged, cutting through the killer's Obituary shirt and leaving a thin line bursting with bright-red blood across his chest. He recoiled, clenching his fists.

The killer ran at Stella. Stella launched toward him. He raised his knife high above his head. Stella turned her knife horizontally, bracing for the impact of blade against blade. With a last-minute jerk, the killer crouched and thrust his knife toward Stella's gut. She clenched, writhing against the momentum of her body, falling toward the tip of the blade.

A glint of light flickered. The killer hunched over, gripping both sides of his upper leg. A whiff of cinnamon jolted Stella as Iris hovered over the man.

Stella grabbed the killer by his hair, whipped his head back and smashed his skull against the crate floor. His eyes rolled back. Iris' knife protruded from the center of his upper thigh, blood blooming through his jeans. Iris retrieved her weapon.

Stella joined Iris beside the victim, who stared at them wildly, as if unable to process the reality of what was happening. Iris grabbed his discarded shirt, helped him to sit up, then wrapped the material around his torso to stop the bleeding from the deadly message.

"Can you stand?" Iris asked the young man.

He nodded and slid off the table. As his feet hit the floor, his knees buckled. Iris grabbed him. As he steadied himself, he nodded.

Iris leaned in toward the man's face and spoke in a nearly demonic tone. "We don't exist. You escaped."

The man stared, perplexed and silent.

"We don't exist. *Say it.*"

He nodded, then whispered, his lower lip quivering. "You...don't...exist." He tried to swallow.

"Now get the fuck out of here." Iris pointed at the door with her knife.

The young man stumbled toward the door and vanished into the darkness. Stella hoped he'd find help before he bled out.

It was time to deal with the Nü-Metal Killer. He lay limp on the floor. Iris walked up to him, clutching her knife high, ready to strike. Stella lunged, grabbing Iris' arm as she swung the blade toward the man's throat.

Iris spun on her heel. "What the *fuck*?"

Facing her dead-on, Stella spoke. "After what you saw, you want to make this easy for him?"

"I want to *kill* him. Isn't that what we set out to do?" Iris raised her eyebrow.

"I have a better idea." Stella licked her lips and slyly walked over to her prey.

Iris watched as Stella slid her hands under the man's armpits and lifted. "Don't you want a piece of him?"

Hesitating, Iris slid her knife into its sheath and helped Stella lift him onto the table. He moaned, slipping in and out of consciousness, as Stella tied his wrists and ankles with wire, then secured him to holes at the head and foot of the table.

Stella positioned herself over the body, knife in hand. As she slid the tip of the blade into the killer's flesh, lustful heat surged through her entire body. She carved the outline of a square across his chest, down to his abdomen, then back up again, preparing her canvas for a message of death metal extremes. She looked up from her work. Iris stared at her, her expression a mixture of unease and confusion.

"Tell me that there is *no part* of you that wants a piece of this." If she did, then this might be the end of their partnership. Stella shook with anticipation. She didn't want their ride to end before their first kill.

Iris swallowed. "I can't tell you that." She unveiled her knife and joined Stella.

They took turns carefully carving the flesh within the perimeter of the canvas that Stella had prepared as she whispered instructions. The Nü-Metal Killer deserved a serving of his own signature. Partway through, his eyes opened fully as consciousness awakened him. He screamed and thrashed against the pain of each slice. It had little impact. They'd tied his limbs tight. He was secure. There was no one for miles and miles. His cries would go unheard.

Their artwork of flesh, a macabre masterpiece, moist and fresh, glowed scarlet under the orange light of the candles. Just like he had, they'd carved three-dimensional letters into his skin and peeled away the square of epidermis, leaving the letters raised from the body. Pink meat protrusions on a ruby-red canvas.

For Vengeance We Scream.

His chest rose and sank in a desperate cycle, gripping his last moments of life. Stella raised her knife, covered in the killer's life juices, and licked the blade from base to tip. Iris looked at her with both shock and curiosity.

As they walked to the door, the killer's raspy voice clawed at them. "You cunts. I'll kill you."

Stella spun on her heel and smirked. "Good luck with that." She blew him a kiss and then left him to die in his death crate.

Chapter 8
Homicidal Ideation

As she took an indulgent pull of the room-temperature bourbon, Stella settled her head back against the thin motel pillow. She closed her eyes. The same montage that assaulted her every night immediately returned. The faces of every victim she'd failed to save stared her down, their black eyes probing into her soul, their blue lips whispering to her. Despite the cold, hard fact that she'd walked away from her detective life, away from the stifling rules imposed by her badge, she wondered if she'd be able to do enough. How many innocent victims bled every moment, everywhere?

The bed creaked as she shifted against the headboard. She shot back the rest of the bourbon in the plastic cup. The empty bottle on the nightstand offered her no solace. She hoped Iris would be back soon from her supply run.

Squeezing her eyes shut harder, she stared at the faces of the dead, watching their mouths open, hearing their haunting whispers. They begged her to save them. Every single one of them was innocent. Leading a life of pure intentions. Not inflicting harm on anyone. Each of them fit the profile of the actor or actress required to play out a psycho fantasy that drove the actions of the sick and deranged. Their innocence sacrificed because Stella wasn't smart enough, fast enough…because she didn't follow the instincts raging in the pit of her gut, screaming through her mind.

Her first kill with Iris by her side had left her higher than any. The exhilaration pumped through her like a shot of heroin. Her desire for blood swelled like an ocean wave.

The face of the young man, the victim of the Nü-Metal Killer, flashed through her mind, wiping away all the other dead eyes staring her down. His screams as he writhed against the steel table still pierced her ears. His expression—the panic, the fear, the *realization* that he was going to die—burned into her soul. The heavy throbbing that took over Stella's body, from her gut, up to her throat, created the *desire* within her to manifest that same expression on the metal maniac's face. To slowly carve his flesh and peel it away from his body. To make him beg for his life, screaming in pain.

She curled forward and stepped off the bed, then paced the room. The crusty carpet scratched her bare feet, reminding her where she was. Running her hand through her greasy hair, she longed for her soft strawberry-blonde curls. Her necessary makeover wore thin.

At first, her kills had been efficient, achieving what was necessary to purge those who killed the innocent. As she migrated south, her methods had morphed. It started with her desire to consume the life juice of her prey. With the Nü-Metal Killer, she'd *needed* to torture him, to make him *feel* what he'd made his victims feel.

A craving was building deep down. She'd walked away from her life to find out who she was. Something within her was morphing, turning her into the very human monsters that she was purging from the earth. A killer of killers.

Her gut screamed with the realization that her purpose was to slaughter as many as she could before she lost her mind or died at the hands of one of them.

INNOCENCE

Chapter 9
Hot and Bothered

Only three cars occupied the parking lot in front of Motel 6. One of them was the golden '73 Ford Mustang they'd ditched the black Trans-Am for before crossing the border into New Mexico. Sometimes, she missed her blue Sunfire. But she'd run from her life, and she didn't want to be found. Plus, they'd left carnage. The last thing she wanted was for this exhilarating killing spree to end.

It was easy convincing the half-stoned teenager behind the front desk of the shitty motel in Mesilla to give them the room at the end, away from anyone else. Stella craved some quiet, and she didn't want anyone to see either of their faces. A single window at the back of the room exposed a view of an open field dotted with wildflowers. Lush green grass and a plethora of floral colours gave Stella a small snippet of comfort, offering a complete juxtaposition from the bloody scene they'd left in their wake.

Room 101 smelled old and forgotten. She wondered how long it had been unoccupied. As she poured a double shot of Wild Turkey into the plastic cup she'd found by the sink in the claustrophobic bathroom, she watched Iris saunter through the bathroom door wearing only a tight tank top and cotton panties, holding a towel to her head, patting her damp hair. A scorching tide of arousal gushed through Stella's extremities. They'd agreed to keep their interactions *professional.*

Stella knew that was the only way for them to stay focused. She also wondered if it was the only way to prevent herself from letting the intoxicating woman in, to keep her emotions locked away as they had been for the twenty-four years of her life. Curiosity simmered as she thought about getting close to Iris. Would it really be a bad idea? Could she, cold-hearted Stella Mahoney, actually care for someone? She shook her head and gulped back half the bourbon in a single shot. It was a hopeless thought. She'd *almost* been close to someone once until she'd purposely sabotaged it. The whole thing had nearly suffocated her. But...*Iris.*

She exhaled and indulged in a long look at the woman, lingering her gaze on Iris' breasts, plump and defying gravity, her nipples, erect and pressing against the thin material of her top, her curvaceous figure, and the spot between her legs nearly visible through the sheer panties.

Stella finished the bourbon and poured another. She needed sexual release, as she always did after a kill. But this time, her lust simmered higher than usual, and she'd have to cool down some other way. The only release she was going to get tonight would be with a cold shower and a sensual massage with her own fingers. They'd made an agreement, and she would stick to it. She couldn't imagine losing Iris now and having to continue this purge on her own. Despite her inability to get close to people, she couldn't deny that nearly two years on the road by herself had her yearning for something...some kind of connection.

She sat up, slid off the bed, bourbon in hand, and walked over to the small table beside the kitchenette where she'd laid out a series of newspaper clippings. If she couldn't devour Iris to ease her sexual energy, she'd focus on feeding her addiction to blood.

On her journey, she'd been collecting newspapers at gas stations, diners, and corner stores. The ones from the small-town presses were the most interesting. They were the ones with hungry, rookie journalists, foaming at the mouth to make it big. They were the ones writing the stories about the goriest murder the off-the-radar town had ever seen. The ones that didn't hold back on the macabre details, unafraid to take ri sks.

There wasn't much cross-town communication out in the open desert where the small dots of civilization spread out, with nothing but cacti and dust in between. Stella clipped out the most interesting articles and started a collection. Patterns appeared. The one she inspected now as she sipped her bourbon slowly, not wanting to get too fuzzy headed until after she'd spent some time on this, was a series of articles about male hikers. They'd gone missing, months apart. They may have all been in the same hiking area, but it was only speculation. All in their twenties, all fit and muscular, and all lone adventurers. They were of various ethnicities, defying the usual victim type. Yet, something tugged at Stella's gut.

Stella sat down at the table, picked up the red marker she'd bought at Sue's Sideroad Store, and snapped the cap off.

Pressing the plastic cup to her lips, only a couple of droplets slid out.

"Refill?" Iris' body heat swelled behind her.

"Of course." Stella forced her body to simmer down as Iris filled her cup.

"When did you get that?" Iris pointed at the symbol inked into Stella's upper arm, three partial circles meeting in the centre. "It's pretty."

Stella looked at the tattoo, the memory of the day she got it blazing bright in her mind. It had been after her first kill as a free agent. "Symbol of purge. Got it when I...started my new journey."

"It suits you." Iris sat beside her, pouring her own drink. "Working on something?"

"Missing hikers. Same age. Same build. Some missing parameters for a full victim type...but I'm sure there's something here."

Iris examined the articles. "Where are these hiking trails?"

"These are only *guesses* where they last were." Stella re-scanned the articles one by one, circling the names of the trails with the marker. Shuffling through the papers, she found the stack of full-sized road maps she'd been collecting.

Stella unfolded the map of New Mexico and spread it out over the table. She circled each of the locations of the hiking trails—*Touch-Me-Not-Mountain, Garcia Peak,* and *Mesa Urraca*—then stood up, sipped her bourbon, and stared at the red circles.

"These are all in Cimarron Canyon State Park," Iris bit her bottom lip and raised an eyebrow.

Forcing herself to focus on the map and not steal a glance at Iris' round ass through the sheer underwear, Stella cleared her mind of lustful thoughts and wrapped her brain around the trail locations.

She ran her finger along the only major road that accessed the state park. "Why isn't there anything along here?"

Gulping the rest of the bourbon in her cup, she savoured the liquid fire and the buzz in her temples. *It's the wrong map.* Rummaging through the stack of maps, she grabbed the one she'd picked up days ago at George's Gas Stop. Different from the standard ones she'd been using, it had caught her eye. She unfolded it and smoothed it out over the table.

"Different map?" Iris inquired.

"Historic map." She examined the legend. "Towns with an X through them don't exist anymore. They don't show up on the standard road maps."

"You're turning into a map geek." Iris chuckled.

"Yeah, well..." She couldn't help but giggle. As she refocused on the map, she fell silent.

"What?" Iris leaned in, her face close to Stella's.

"Cimarron." She pointed at a dot with an X through it. The three hiking trails formed a semicircle around it.

"So, it's not a town anymore?" Iris asked.

"No, it's not." She smiled as she pointed at the legend on the right side of the map. "Declared a ghost town."

"Deserted." Iris sat back against the chair slyly. She pulled her knee to her chest, her legs spreading slightly.

Stella choked back a gasp. Even an ice bath wouldn't save her now. "Perfect for a predator of young, fit men."

"Looks like we're taking a drive to *no one fucking lives here.*" Iris smirked playfully.

Stella took a deep breath, refilled her cup, and resisted the temptation of cinnamon and cherry lips.

Chapter 10
Terrorizer

Dust swirled in clouds as the golden Mustang flew down the deserted dirt road. "Superterrorizer" by *Black Label Society* blasted from the speakers. The guitar shot electric chords like bullets, piercing the front cab with sharp punches of sound. Mr. Wylde's gritty metal voice savagely told them they were suicidal doomsday machines. Iris, eyes closed, white-blonde hair pressed into the headrest, tapped her fingers against the window, synchronized with the thrumming bass beat. Stella breathed in the dry, musty air through the open window, her black hair flapping around erratically. She ached to terrorize.

Cimarron came into view. On the northern tip of New Mexico, only the dead souls of long-gone coal miners inhabited the ghost town. A series of young men, adventurers, were missing. They may all have been hiking in Cimarron Canyon State Park before they disappeared. The trifecta of mountain ranges formed a semicircle around Cimarron. Speculation of where grown men, lone travellers known for slipping off the radar, went wasn't enough for the authorities to care. Stella smelled a killer, and she definitely cared.

The victims had a type. Early twenties. Male. Fit. Bearded. Young, vibrant, virile mountain men. Who was this hunter, and what was it about their prey that piqued their senses? Was it a desire to slice open their skin, glowing with youth? Was it sexual, a washed-up loner seeking physical touch but rejected by humanity, having to force it to get satisfaction? Or was it some traumatic event of the past that dominated their every move, forcing them to replay the event over and over, each time needing the perfect actor for their main character?

Stella's feral hunting instincts didn't know or care. What mattered to her was that young men had gone missing, and no one else gave a flying fuck. No one else had the motivation, the resources or, *more importantly,* the balls to find the psycho taking these young men.

At the perimeter of the empty town, Stella turned down the volume on the aggressive song and eased her pressure on the gas pedal. The Mustang slowed to a crawl. The engine quieted. Next to a crumbling saloon, she put the car in park, killed the engine, and glanced at her partner. Iris sat up, slid her knife into its sheath, and nodded.

It was time.

They eased the doors open silently, leaving them ajar, and trudged along the main street, looking for any sign of life. A scream echoed through the thick silence of the dead town. The voice of a man in despair. A cry of pain so intense—the result of a sadistic act.

Stella halted, spun on her heel, cocked her head, and waited.

Another screech pierced the thick, hot air. She turned toward the source, down a stretch of road. At the end, a brown brick building stood, chunks of concrete crumbling around its base, its blackened windows staring at them like demon eyes. A sign hung crooked on its hinges. *Aztec Mill Museum.*

Stella led the way, Iris on her heels. They slid their knives from their cases and clutched them, ready to drink in the flowing blood, to breathe in death and decay, and to gut a killer.

Chapter 11
Red Room

The door to the abandoned mill was so far into decay that a double-booted kick was completely unnecessary. Iris smirked, held up three fingers, and gave their customary countdown. Stella pushed the door open with a gentle tap. It creaked loudly. She cringed, hoping the noise wouldn't alert their target.

The odour hit them immediately. Death. Rot. Human juices. Fecal matter. All mixed into a spoiled cocktail of filth. They stood at the edge of the doorway. The space ate up every beam of sunlight, swallowing it into a pit of darkness.

Stella grabbed her flashlight from her belt, clicked it on, and bathed the room in white light, starting with the wall to the left. Viscous red liquid oozed down the wooden planks. Chunks of flesh piled along the perimeter, forming human meat mounds along the scarlet wall. Guiding the light to the far corner, she exposed the back wall. Her fingers grasped the flashlight harder as the horror came alive.

Bodies. Bloody, decaying bodies, hanging from hooks lodged in the back of their skulls.

Iris released a tiny gasp, then fell silent, composing herself.

Stella continued to move the light along the line of bodies, silently counting to herself. One. Two. Three. Four. Five. *Six.*

Six bloody bodies, hanging like hunted carcasses, in various stages of decay. All young men, lean and muscular. All with beards. She'd nailed the victim type. These had to be the missing hikers. Her instincts screamed in the pit of her gut.

Choking back a ball of bile and undigested greasy steak and eggs, Stella exhaled through her nose. She'd seen and smelled a lot. This had to be up there with the grossest scenes she'd absorbed. She guided the light down one body. Mounds of maggots crawled inside his open chest. Chunks of flesh hung by thin threads of skin. Where his sexual organs should be, only a gaping red hole remained.

"What the *fuck?*" Stella whispered hoarsely as she lit up the open excavation of his missing manhood.

"Jesus Christ," Iris murmured.

The light exposed the corpse's legs, strips of flesh torn away, tendons and bones exposed. On the floor, between what remained of his dangling feet, sat a pile of red, shredded meat, with a pinkish cylindrical chunk of flesh on top. It looked like a mutilated penis. What *the hell* had happened here?

As she exhaled, Stella stole a glance at Iris. Iris frowned deeply.

Investigating the wall to the right revealed more blood, guts, and flesh. Had these piles of human parts been other bodies? How many slaughtered missing hikers were in this red room?

A wretched cry came from the far-right corner. Stella shot the light toward the scream. A door bathed in gore and smeared in guts, heavy metal and solid on its hinges, blocked them from the horrors beyond.

Stella made eye contact with Iris. Iris nodded. They moved toward the door in unison.

Adjusting to the retched stench, the bath of blood smeared on every surface, tingles erupted down Stella's arms and through her stomach. Heat ran through her veins. The knife shook as her hand trembled, ready to slice and dice. The zest of a kill clung to the back of her tongue. Electric sparks ignited every nerve ending as she imagined the blade opening flesh as she looked into the crazed eyes of the person responsible for this slaughter.

They reached the door. Stella clicked off the light and hooked it to her belt. Iris raised her fingers for the next countdown.

Chapter 12
Carnal Cougar

The door swung open in silence. A killer executing victims in a ghost town didn't have to worry about locking the door to their dungeon. Until Stella and Iris showed up.

Stella entered first, Iris close behind. They stood in silence, mesmerized by the scene before them. A curvaceous woman, encased in black leather so tight, nearly bursting at the seams like an overstuffed pork sausage, mounted upon the rock-hard cock of a man, his erection sliding in and out of her through a circular opening in the crotch of her pants.

Stunned into paralysis, Stella stared. Iris fell silent beside her.

The woman had her back to them. Her auburn curls fell in a great wave down her back, flipping from side to side as she rode the man raw. Her shiny black boots secured on two metal steps, like the stirrups used to position the entry into a female for a pap smear. In each hand, she gripped a leather strap secured to the wall.

The man moaned in pain, screamed in agony, his head lolled back. With his arms stretched up over his head, his wrists were raw and bleeding from the binds digging into his flesh. The woman thrust upward, preparing herself for penetration, exposing the man's genitals. A metal ring wrapped around the base of his cock. Heavy metal balls hung from his testicles, stretching them into thin strips. Blood poured from open tears and oozed over his thick pubic hair.

The man's face fell forward, his eyes rolling back in his head. The woman raised her arm, clutching a long metal rod in her hand.

"Don't you dare," her shrill voice pierced the room.

She pressed the end of the rod into the side of the man's torn neck. A buzzing sound erupted, like an electrical current, and the man's body convulsed in a grotesque seizure. His eyes flung open. He howled louder than ever. His jawline clenched. Blood spurted from his wrists as he strained them against the bindings.

"You'll make me cum harder than a porn star," she screeched.

The buzzing halted. The woman pressed her vaginal cavity over his penis, her hole devouring his cock like a hungry animal. She arched her back and pumped harder and faster, thrusting him so deep inside of her that sanguine fluid trickled down her legs, sliding down the shiny leather and splatting over the floor. Her speed increased so tremendously that his right testicle tore clean off and landed with a loud, bloody splat.

He screamed like a wild animal.

Stella bit her bottom lip. Rage consumed her. Something animalistic swelled within. A craving for the metallic tang of blood on her tongue took over.

"Fucking yes!" The woman's entire body shuddered in a massive convulsion.

She threw her head back and moaned, her eyes closed, her cheeks moist with sweat. Crow's feet crinkled the sides of her eyes, her face etched with time and experience.

"Carnal Cougar," Stella whispered.

Iris smirked.

The killer grabbed the leather straps and dismounted, one leg at a time. Facing her lustful prey, she fluffed up her hair and purred like a mountain cat. The man's head lolled forward as he whimpered, and his eyelids fluttered and closed.

As the Carnal Cougar stepped to the side, still facing her victim of lust, the man's body came into full view. His mutilated cock, ripped to shreds, was a pathetic representation of what it had once been. The magnificent girth of his penis was still apparent, despite the missing strips of flesh, and the sheen of bright red blood that dripped from its still hardened state, forced by the tight, metal ring around its base. The single ball that remained stretched paper thin with the metal sphere still attached. It clung to his groin by a nearly transparent thread of skin, and it was a mangled, gory, deformed shape. He bled profusely from the slit where his other testicle had been prior to ripping clean off. It now lay in a fleshy, gruesome lump beneath him. Red juice stained his leg in a steady stream.

The gaping hole in the body hanging in the other room flashed in Stella's mind. All these men had clearly bled to death after their sick sexual encounter with this deranged, oversexed female. She had a type. Young, muscular, fit, and hung like a horse.

Stella gritted her teeth, fighting the sexual heat building in her loins, chalking it off as a normal reaction to seeing such a blood-filled live smut scene. The physical wiring of humans causes them to have reactions beyond their control. That's all it was.

She gripped her knife and glanced at Iris. Seeing that her partner in murder was as ready as she was, she took several silent steps toward the sexually satisfied killer. Iris followed suit.

They were merely three feet away when the Carnal Cougar turned around.

The woman gasped, then immediately changed her expression to one of pure, sadistic delight. "Well, well...what do we have here?" She licked her lips like a lioness about to feed.

"Not another step, bitch," Stella spat as she raised her knife.

"Mmm...you gonna...*cut* me?" Her nostrils flared.

Iris moved in before Stella could answer, raising her leg in a brutal kick right into the killer's groin. The woman slammed against the wall. She smothered her hands in the gore dripping down the wet surface.

"You like the taste of blood?" She brought her hand to her face and licked herself from her wrist to the tip of her middle finger.

Iris lunged, then slid her blade up the killer's arm. Blood spurted from the gash. The woman spun, raising her leg into a high kick. The sharp heel of her boot connected with Iris' face, leaving a deep gash along her cheekbone. Iris took several quick steps backward, dropping her knife, and nearly falling. Stella swiped her blade through the moist, metallic air as she lunged forward. The woman cowered back. Steel sliced clean across her chin. Her hand sprang to her face.

"You evil bitch." She took several steps forward. "Who the *fuck* do you think you are?"

Stella stood her ground, worming forward, her face inches from the woman's. "Your date with death."

The woman laughed. "Not in this lifetime, honey." Her arm came around, her fist catching Stella's left cheek in a nasty right hook. Recoiling from the impact, her grip on the wooden handle loosened as shook her head. The Beast Hunter clattered to the ground. With a clenched fist, Iris punched the Carnal Cougar square in the nose. Cartilage cracked. An eruption of red oozed from the woman's nostrils. She reeled backward.

"Fucking Bitch!" A pool of blood formed in the woman's hand as she cupped her crushed nasal canal. Blood sprayed as she whipped her hand away and sprinted forward, screeching like a banshee.

Iris kicked the woman's shin. She stumbled, maintaining tremendous momentum. With a full body twist, Stella thrust her elbow into the woman's gut.

The woman spat a mixture of blood, mucus, and saliva as she clutched her gut. She refused to go down. Her eyes narrowed as she raised her leg high and twirled her body in a feat of gymnastic athleticism. Her boot smashed Stella's cheekbone. Fluids flew from the opening in the woman's crotch, splatting against Stella's throbbing face. Liquid oozed down her skin, trickling over the corner of her mouth. The taste of the ejaculate of a man who'd eaten a coconut lingered on her lips.

"Enough." Stella flung her weight against the vile woman's body.

The woman stumbled backward. Stella continued to push with all her might until the woman's back hit the bloody wall. Red droplets flew, landing on Stella's face. Stella thrust her elbow against the woman's jaw. Bones cracked. The woman blinked rapidly, struggling to focus. A glint of light revealed

Stella's knife, a few inches to her right. She grabbed and stabbed it up between the woman's legs, slicing into the open hole in the leather pants. The point of the blade pierced the woman's left lip, then sliced it open, from back to front.

The killer screeched. "You motherfucking monster!"

She hunched forward, clutching her crotch with both hands, blood pouring in a fast stream. She fell to her knees, stretching her hands out in front of her. Blood dripped from her trembling fingers.

"What have you done?" Her lower lip trembled. Spit dribbled down her chin.

"Cut you where it counts." Stella stepped back and held up her knife, the blade coated in the woman's vaginal juices.

Iris, with a look of shock on her face, stepped forward and kicked the woman's shoulder, causing her to slump over on her side. Stella pressed her own boot into the woman's other shoulder, holding her against the floor.

A glitch shook the room. Blood poured from the woman's crotch into a massive red pool. Her screams rang loud. The world spun. Stella blinked rapidly, trying to focus. The puddle of blood was gone. The killer lay on her side, pinned by Iris and Stella's boots.

Stella crouched, pinning her prey's knees and pointing her blade toward the woman's crotch. "Had enough? Or shall we continue?"

Anger seethed in the woman's eyes. "Fuck you, cunt." More spit dribbled from the corner of her mouth.

Iris moved behind the woman's head, then positioned one knee over each of the woman's shoulders, pressing her against the floor. Stella straddled her.

"Get the fuck off me. You sluts!" The woman's body spasmed as she tried to break free.

"Now, now, quiet down," Iris coaxed.

A tremor wove through Stella. Her body quivered. Hot tingles erupted in her gut. She swallowed against the mix of lust, excitement, and hatred soaring up her throat. Parting the woman's legs, Stella slid her knees further down the woman's body, pinning her prey by the shins. She exhaled slowly, steadying her hand, then pointed the tip of the blade just inside the woman's pussy. Her prey squirmed. Stella imagined great waves of blood. She licked her lips as she slid the blade right into the killer's vaginal cavity.

The woman wailed like a banshee. Blood poured from the moist hole down the handle of the knife and over Stella's hand. Her fingers, now inside the woman as she slid the knife in further. She twisted the knife, cutting through internal flesh. The woman's screeches reached a higher decibel, piercing Stella's eardrums. As she pulled the blade from between the woman's legs, feminine fluids and scarlet mucus coated her fingers. The woman kicked wildly and writhed beneath Iris' grip. Iris released her, stood, and looked down at the shell of a killer, bleeding profusely from her sexual core.

Stella crawled up beside the woman and moved in close enough for the woman's hot breath to touch her face. Gripping the handle of her knife hard, Stella brought the blade up to her mouth. She ran her tongue from the base of the steel up to the tip, then swallowed back the mix of sex and death. A slight tropical after-taste lingered.

As she looked the woman in the eyes, she whispered, "Your rot tastes sweet."

Stella stood up and stepped back. Iris stared at her in shock.

The woman winced, curled into the fetal position, and whimpered softly. Blood soaked her legs and pooled around her.

Stella cleaned the blade of her knife with the bottom of her shirt and then slid it into its leather sheath. Iris cleaned and secured her own knife, leaving a stain of red on the hem of her thin top.

The ravaged young man, still hanging by his wrists, appeared lifeless. Stella stepped up to him, pressed two fingers to his wrist, confirming that he had slipped away. She shook her head, knowing it was for the best.

Side by side, Stella and Iris walked to the metal door. As they re-entered the blood-bathed room full of rotting carcasses, pairs of black eyes stared them down. Stella couldn't help but examine every detail etched into their corpses, remnants of the most savage sexual encounter of their lives as they succumbed to the darkness.

Chapter 13
Killing Time

Her fist hit the mirror. A jagged spiderweb pattern crackled through the glass. Shards fell and clinked against the sink. Blood trickled down her wrist, droplets landing on the white porcelain, spreading like desperate, bloody fingers. *Dammit. What had she done?*

She'd tried *three* times. Nothing worked.

Stella stared at her cracked reflection through the steam filling the small bathroom as the hot shower ran on full blast. A serrated line broke her face in two, reminding her of what she once was, and of what she had become. The crazed look of a feral being stared back at her. Rot festered in her core. The fetid stench of her soul turned fouler with every kill.

She turned up the volume of the boombox wedged against the back of the counter. "Just Killing Time" by *Black Label Society* blasted from the speakers. If Iris returned before she finished, she didn't want to be heard. She'd rubbed her clitoris until it was nearly raw. She'd even inserted several fingers inside herself, trying desperately to climax. Without a release, she couldn't focus on the next kill. The next kill was imperative for the purge. Without it, this would be for nothing. Every time she came close, a yearning for hot pain and the metallic zing of blood took over, causing her near eruption to freeze.

The electric guitar cried like a weeping soul. Melodic piano chords provided a soulful background. The sorrow-filled voice reminded her she was no longer killing time, that time was killing her.

Her bloody fingers clawed at her broken reflection and then grasped a fragment of glass from the sink. It wasn't expiration that she was looking for. She'd faced that long ago, holding her own hunting knife to her neck, teetering on the line between life and death. If she didn't get a release soon, she would go insane, burst from the inside, her mind causing her to do even crazier things than she'd already done. She *had to do this.*

More blood ruptured from her fingers and spilled over her trembling hand as she pointed the piece of glass to the side of her abdomen. She slid her hand inside her panties, finding her sweet spot. As she massaged herself savagely, she pressed the sharpened tip to her skin. A droplet of blood burst free and trickled down the curve of her hip.

Molten desire coursed through her veins. Tingles built. Tremors ran through her. Digging the glass apex into her flesh, she dragged it along the contour of her hipbone, ripping open the skin. Blood oozed down the curve of her body, soaking into the band of her cotton underwear. White pain seared through her, igniting a fresh wave of lustful mini-eruptions.

She raised her hand, dripping with carnage and gripping the jagged wedge, to her mouth. Cotton, moist with her own blood, stuck to her other hand as she increased the pressure against her hardening clit.

She licked the glass, lapping up the liquid. The edge caught her tongue, causing a tiny cut and a slight sting. Blood trickled to the back of her throat, poking the fire building inside of her.

She averted her gaze, not wanting to see herself, her desperate state of needing to cut herself so she could experience a sexual release. Killing and fucking had become one. She couldn't climax unless she was in pain with the taste of blood saturating her tongue. The lunacy of it all both excited and sickened her.

With her eyes clamped shut, she threw her head back and pressed the razor-sharp point against the side of her neck, away from the carotid artery. It poked into her flesh, a blazing sting shaking her senses.

Her fingers worked aggressively between her legs. She was so close, begging silently for the release to come. As desperation nearly drowned her, a climax finally sent trembles through her body.

The glass shard fell into the sink with a loud clink and broke into two pieces. She gripped the sides of the sink with both hands, breathless and spent.

As she opened her eyes, the room whirled, her brain dizzy from the lustful explosion.

She stared again at herself, her broken reflection in the shattered mirror. The ragged cut ran an inch down the curve of her hip. She could hide it. Keep it for her eyes only. The resulting scar would make her look as ugly as she felt inside.

Chapter 14
Creature Corpse

Stella closed her eyes as she tilted her face toward the hot water, letting it wash away the slaughter and the guilt. Clouds of steam filled the entire bathroom, shutting out reality. She ran her fingers along her self-inflicted cut. The hemorrhaging had slowed to a trickle, but it still stung like hell. It was worth it. Calm had taken over her. Her mind was clear. She could focus on planning the next hunt.

She turned off the water, wrapped her hair in a towel and her body in another, then turned down the music still blasting from the boom box. When she opened the door, Iris was sitting at the table, sipping a bourbon, and staring intently at a newspaper. Without looking up, Iris poured a double shot into a plastic cup and pulled out a chair. Stella sat down, gulped back half the liquor, then inspected the article that had Iris' full attention.

"Look at this." Iris slid the paper closer to Stella. "Jesus. You look pale."

Hoping Iris wouldn't catch on to her cutting, Stella attempted a smile. "Just tired. That was intense."

"It was." Iris bit her lip, holding back.

"Thanks for the drink." Stella attempted to change the topic. "How does your face feel?"

Iris touched the adhesive strip along her cheekbone. "Still stings like hell, but it's closing."

Relief had washed through Stella when the bleeding had eased and what initially looked like a deep gash turned out to be a surface wound.

Iris reached over and grazed Stella's bruised cheek with her fingertips. "The swelling has gone down a bit."

Stella recoiled, too depleted to be touched. Even by Iris. "Yeah. It's fine."

"Look at this." Iris pointed at a photo beside the small print.

"Is that..." Stella leaned closer, peering at the photo. It had to be human, but, well, she wasn't sure. "Is that a person?"

"The body of a young girl, apparently. Found behind the campground at Deseret Peak. In Utah. Skin stretched out and stitched."

"This can't be a first kill. I mean...look at it." Stella shot back the other half of the bourbon.

"I made a call." Iris sat back against the chair, waiting for Stella's reaction.

"Risky." Stella poured another round for both of them.

"I used the burner I grabbed at that last gas station. Called someone specific. Someone I trust. Wanted to know if there were other bodies like this."

"And?"

"Two. Both in Wisconsin, in the wilderness. One in Chequamegon-Nicolet National Forest. The other near Clam Lake. Months apart. Ten years ago." Iris tucked a stray strand of hair behind her ear. "Different victim types. One male, twenty-one years old. A woman, thirty-two. After that, nothing."

"No clear link...except the skin?" Stella asked.

"You got it. The skin on both was suspiciously silky. *Velvety,* says here. Swabs showed high levels of dimethicone. Alters the texture. Makes it malleable."

Stella scanned the article. "The skin on this new body also had nitrocellulose. Used in lacquers. Finishing for furniture, nail polish, *leather.*"

"Fuck. What was this killer *making*?" Iris grimaced.

"Don't know. But we're gonna find out." Stella got up from the chair and paced across the room.

"Hey, my colleague mentioned the forensic chemist from your last case...Brad? No, Bryce. He called, looking for me." Iris raised an eyebrow.

"Oh...really?" Stella played coy.

"He wasn't looking for *me*, was he?" Iris smirked. "I barely spoke to the guy. But...you spent some time in his lab, didn't you?"

Heat flushed Stella's face at the thought of Bryce, his amber eyes, his dark hair, his tongue on her skin. "I guess. Part of the case."

"You're avoiding my gaze. You do that when you're holding back." Iris twisted in her chair.

Stella slipped a t-shirt over her head and dropped the wet towel onto the floor. "Not avoiding you. Just getting cold." She hoped the cut had clotted and wouldn't bleed through.

Iris pulled the paper back toward her. "I know we've been following your gut. Mine is telling me *this* is our next one."

"Mine says the same thing." Stella walked back to the table, poured a fresh drink and sauntered over to the bed. "We should try to sleep. Hit the road early. We need to go check out the location they found the body. Killer might be lingering."

"Good call." Iris tipped her plastic cup toward Stella in a toast to their next hunt.

Chapter 15
Chicken Coop

A red glow scintillated through the dive joint. A shabby-looking rock ensemble sauntered lazily across the stage at the front. The gritty voice of the lead singer added an edge to the smooth guitar riffs and by-the-book drumbeat. Stella leaned into the cracked wood of the back of the chair and rested her left boot over her right knee. Pain throbbed along her hip. She bit her lip, stifling a gasp, then took a long pull of the double bourbon that Iris had set in front of her.

They'd left early, before sunrise, and driven all day. The photo of the young girl, her skin softened, stretched, and sewn, was enough to convince Stella to move on without a break. Besides, they needed to put some distance between them and the bloody mess they'd made of the Carnal Cougar. The mess that *she'd* made while Iris looked at her in shock. Tired, hot, and thirsty, they agreed to stop for the night and hit the road again early in the morning. It was easier to cover more ground before the sun lit up and cooked the open desert roads. Looking for some liquor relief on the outskirts of Colorado Springs, the sign out front of the *Chicken Coop* promised cute chicks and cheap booze.

Iris leaned close, talking over the music. "I can't stop thinking about the photo. The girl...she was...she didn't look human."

"I know." Stella nearly closed her eyes as she breathed in Iris' sweet aroma. Pain thrummed in her hip, reminding her of where her sexual desires took her and distinguishing her lust. "The three bodies—they're connected."

"But why after ten years? And why halfway across the country?" Iris sipped her drink, her cherry lips dipping sexily into the amber liquid.

"What's the connection between Wisconsin and Utah? Is there even one?" Stella slipped several folded maps from the inner pocket of her jacket.

"New ones?" Iris raised an eyebrow. "You are officially a map geek."

"Grabbed them while you were in the restroom at the last gas station." Stella spread them out on the table. "This one's a standard road map, but it's old. This one is another historic map. Both might show us places that are now abandoned. And *this* one," she tapped it with her finger, "is a treasure. A military topographic map. This guy had a bunch of them in his store. I wonder where he got them."

"Military?" Iris asked.

"We need to find out what would take the killer across the country. Might be something on this map that wasn't on the others. The skin. The stitches. First two bodies *have* to be connected to this third." She unfolded the map to expose the Western desert.

Iris exhaled as she leaned back against the chair. "High levels of dimethicone on all three. Nitrocellulose on the new one. Lubing and polishing the skin, turning it into human leather."

Stella pointed at Deseret Peak on the map. "Girl's body was found here."

"Nothing but mountains," Iris noted.

"And open desert." A square outline grabbed her attention. She pointed at it. "This wasn't on the other maps. Dugway Proving Ground."

"Some kind of military base?" Iris inspected the legend on the map.

"Seems like it." Stella tensed her jaw as she ran her finger down the symbols. "Chemical test site. In the heart of the base."

"You thinking what I'm thinking?" Iris tapped her fingernails on the table.

"A killer with a forte for chemicals might have a connection to this place. I want to know what goes on at this site. We need more information." Iris chugged her bourbon. "First, we need another round and an attempt at sleep."

"Definitely." Stella crinkled her nose. "And a hot shower. I stink."

Chapter 16
Brad's Bytes

It was hot and stuffy in the cafe. Sweat pooled down the curve of Stella's back as she leaned in toward the computer screen. Now on a full hunt for the killer leaving bodies with elastic skin slathered up like leather, they'd left the motel down the street from the Chicken Coop in Colorado Springs before sunrise.

After shooting north on the number twenty-five highway, Stella turned west onto the eighty. The quickest route to get to Salt Lake City. After hours of driving, Stella desperately needed to stop and clear her head, to make sense of the ideas swirling through her brain at hurricane speed. The multiple double bourbons last night had left a slight throbbing at the back of her skull. When she saw the sign for Bitter Creek, she chose a slight detour off the eighty down Bitter Creek Road. As she drove into the small town, she spotted the sign for Brad's Bytes, promising strong coffee and the fastest dial-up Internet in Wyoming. It was a tall order for a tiny town in the middle of nowhere, but she needed a break and some answers. She hoped Brad would deliver.

Iris, sitting next to her, clicked away at the keys, the odour of disinfectant wafting from the keyboard. Brad kept his shop, and the computers lining the table along the wall, in good condition. Hot air blew past her from the fan spinning in the computer at her station. It was only the two of them, and a scraggly-looking teenager in the corner, manically pressing the buttons of a game controller attached to the computer he was facing.

Behind the counter, Brad focused intently on a magazine, flipping pages as he sipped from a mug plastered with the pixelated cafe logo. Casually, she slipped a flask from her back pocket, unscrewed the lid, and took an ample swig. The burn numbed her throat and eased the thrumming in her skull. Researching in public seemed risky, but they needed information, and this place was off the radar. They needed the power of the World Wide Web and the abilities of the Google Search Engine. Brad had eagerly accepted cash, hadn't asked questions, and paid little attention to them.

She finished typing in a search for chemical testing at the Dugway Proving Ground and hit enter. Neon-green text slowly filled the screen. She willed the results to give her the nugget of information that would make her gut tingle. The thought of another swig of bourbon crossed her mind, but Brad glanced their way. The limited menu only offered coffee in several forms, nothing strong enough to satiate Stella's thirst. Looking bored, Brad returned his attention to his magazine, flipping a page as if he'd rather be somewhere else.

"Get anything?" Iris asked.

Teiko chemical testing site, flashed at the top of the screen in lime green.

Stella quickly scanned the information. "Teiko chemical test site. Part of the military base. Nestled in the Great Salt Lake desert. Established during the Second World War. Open-air chemical and biological testing site. High-hazard and explosive tests. Shut down eleven years ago."

"Abandoned?" Iris asked.

"Looks like it. Actually, looks like most of the base is." Stella clicked on a link.

A page titled *Johnny Film Man's LiveJournal* filled up the screen. Photos popped up showing the decrepit state of the deserted test site. Rooms full of old computers and tables cluttered with piles of yellowing papers. Bunker-style tunnels. Laboratories with rusting tables and rows upon rows of dust-covered vials and jars.

"Is that actual footage?" Iris slid her chair closer.

"Some guy named Johnny went in there. A filmmaker looking for a post-apocalyptic vibe. He put his photos, and even some snippets of his film, up here on his production journal." She clenched her jaw as she zoomed in on a photo of the jars and vials. "Look at this."

Despite the dust, the words on the labels clearly read nitroglycerine, ammonium perchlorate, and nitrocellulose. "Bingo."

"Is there more?" Iris asked.

Stella scrolled through the text. "Says here he wasn't the only one to go in there. Bunch of links."

"What do they lead to?" Iris' knee shook.

"Double bingo." Stella hovered the pointer on the screen over a link.

Mad Scientist at Teiko Test Range under Investigation.

"Click on it." Iris' eyes widened.

Stella clicked. The computer whirred, shooting off another blast of hot air. Several black-and-white news articles lit up the screen. She sifted through them, then came to a sudden halt and zoomed in.

Salt Lake Sizzler. June 20, 1983.

Doctor Mill Mortem, a senior chemical specialist at the Teiko Test Site, was relieved of his duties. Because of the extreme experiments that Dr. Mortem was conducting in an unused bunker, a full investigation is underway. Preliminary testing on the domestic pigs found in cages in the bunker has revealed a concoction of toxic and flammable chemicals in their skin. The texture of the skin has led to the inference that Dr. Mortem was trying to make it malleable. Upon questioning, he has refused to reveal the purpose of his experiments.

"This *has* to be our killer. What was he doing out east? What made him come back after all this time?" Iris rambled on.

Stella tuned her out and rapidly scanned the article. "Oh, my god."

"What?" Iris fell silent.

Stella clicked on another link. Another article appeared, plastered with photos of a young girl.

"They found his daughter, Catrina, locked in a cage in the back of the deserted bunker where he was experimenting on the pigs." Stella swallowed, aching for a full double bourbon right about now.

"Her skin..." Iris stared at the photos, mouth ajar. "It looks like stretched leather."

Stella scrolled down the article, revealing additional photos. A large tank of water perched beside the girl in the cage. "What the *hell* would that be for?"

"His own child turned into a human test subject," Iris whispered.

"What was he trying to *make?*" Stella's heart tightened and her gut throbbed.

"Where is he now?" Iris asked.

Stella typed his name in and watched the results pour across the screen. "Died. 1991. February 12."

"Just before the discovery of the first two bodies." Iris sighed.

"The daughter..." Stella typed in *Catrina Mortem.*

An article from the *Glidden Golden*, dated February 15, 1991, depicted the photo of a young woman at a gravesite. Her long hair and wide-brimmed black hat concealed her face. "Catrina. Attending her father's funeral. Says she had no other relatives." Stella scrolled through the text.

"What happened to her when they found her in the cage?" Iris asked.

Stella sifted through the data. "There's nothing else about her. It's like she vanished."

"The two bodies were discovered *after* the funeral," Iris stated. "Close to Glidden."

"But they weren't fresh," Stella said.

"So, what? She was the subject of her father's sick experiments. He's discharged, releasing her from her cage. Time passes. Daughter is all grown up. She watches poor Daddy die. She tried to take over his legacy, but needed practice to perfect her methods, and ended up discarding a couple of *failed experiments.* Or Daddy conducted a couple of poor experiments before he ended up six feet under." Iris sat back in her chair, her mouth twisting in contemplation.

"There's an obvious progression between those two and this new one. It could have been her. She improved her skills with the texture of the skin. And with sewing the prepped flesh." Noticing Brad was helping another customer who'd just entered the cafe, Stella snuck another pull of liquor. A pleasant numbness relaxed the tension in her shoulders.

"Maybe...the grief took over. She empathized with her dead dad? Despite her twisted relationship with him, or because of it, she had some sort of *need* to carry on his work?" Iris contemplated.

Stella understood the desire of a girl for a strong father figure. The last serial killer she'd chased as a detective was a young woman following her grandfather's torture techniques. Stella's own father had always been slightly out her reach despite how much she'd ached to be closer to him. He'd been occupied as a homicide detective chasing down serial killers until one of them killed him. "She travels back to where his experiments started. Where her experience with them began." Stella rubbed circles on her temples. Was this too far-fetched?

"Either way. We need to go there and check this out," Iris said.

"Even if she isn't there..." Stella's arms prickled.

"We might find something left behind that can help us out." Iris tapped the table with her fingernails.

Stella nodded. "We might walk into a bounty of behavioural clues." Her brain buzzed, her shoulders clenched, and her boot tapped against the ground.

The thought of looking into Catrina Mortem's eyes, injecting her with a higher dose of nitrocellulose than she'd used on her victims, of peeling away her skin from her bones and morphing her into a more grotesque *thing* than she'd ever created, made Stella's brain buzz. Her craving for the torture, for the kill, for the look in the eyes of someone in excruciating pain was increasing by the second. Maybe intensifying the next slaughter would increase her pleasure and satisfaction.

Iris tapped her shoulder. "Stella. Earth to Stella."

Stella shook her head, dissolving the images of stretching skin. "Sorry."

"I keep losing you. I don't know where you go, but it seems to happen frequently." Iris frowned. "So, Teiko it is, then?" She raised her eyebrow.

"Teiko it is." Stella glanced across the room as she slipped her flask from her pocket.

Chapter 17
Wasteland

The barren desert stretched out in all directions. A vast, open, brown nothingness. Stella hated being so exposed. Their research showed that the Teiko test site was vacant, along with most of the over eight-hundred-thousand-acre military base. Yet, the sense of being watched descended upon her.

Iris walked close beside her, their hips nearly touching. Knives drawn, dead bushes crackling under their dirt-dusted boots, they stalked toward a series of circular, rusted tunnels. Stella peered into a dark opening. Black water dripped from the ceiling. Clumps of mold clung to the sides of the tunnel, stretching green, slimy fingers over the grooves in the metal. A mildewy scent wafted from within the darkness.

She unclipped her flashlight and shone it down the tunnel. They walked in silence, except for the splashes their boots made in the black puddles of muck. When they reached the end, light welcomed them to the other side. The tunnel opened up onto another vast stretch of barren desert. Across the way, a crooked building with dented walls looked to be their next target of exploration. A tilted sign clung to the door by a single rusted nail.

Equipment Bunker.

Stella pulled at the handle. The door creaked loudly, piercing the silence. As she guided her light over the walls, the roof, and the floor, a toxic odour assaulted her senses. She swallowed against her gag reflex and pulled her shirt up over her nose.

"Bloody hell, that's awful," she whispered.

Iris grimaced as she pulled her own shirt over her nostrils. "Smells toxic. Like chemicals."

Poisonous or not, there was no turning back.

Black water dripped down the crusty walls. Droplets fell from the roof, hitting the puddles along the floor with a constant *drip-drip*. Ripples circled through the puddles, making the floor look alive. Stella cautiously placed her steps around the pools, attempting to avoid clicking her heels against the pavement. The place looked like it should be cold, yet a moist heat clung to her skin, causing sweat to break out over her forehead and drizzle down her face. She blinked against the precipitation blurring her vision and focused on guiding the light one step at a time.

If there was anyone in here, they definitely didn't expect to be found.

They reached the end of the room. Stella opened another door, revealing an abandoned workstation of some sort. A wall of computer screens glared down at them like rows of blackened robot eyes. Piles of folders, yellowed and torn papers and files spilling out of them, cluttered a row of desks. Boxes filled with computer equipment, cables and sockets, lined the two side walls.

They manoeuvred through the clutter to another door across the room. A veil of dust fell from the ceiling, coating the sweat still drizzling down Stella's face. She wiped her eyes with her bare arm, continuing to guide them with the light.

The room appeared to be some sort of test laboratory. Filthy glass beakers and tubes lined silver tables crusted in browned, dried fluids. Bunsen burners and torches perched along the backs of the counters, leaning against the stained walls. All kinds of bottles, still half filled with liquids and toxic substances, filled the room—the remnants of chemical experiments to find the most effective way to blow things up.

A cold, deadly vibe percolated through the silent space.

Stella couldn't imagine what went on here. Iris tapped her shoulder and pointed to the far corner of the room where yet another door beckoned them. Stella led the way, pointing her light. When they reached the door, something told her to kill the light, so she did. She secured it to her belt, gripped her Beast Hunter with one hand, and turned the cold, gritty knob with the other.

The door, silent on its still-greased hinges, swung open slowly.

Stella's brain seized.

Chapter 18
Laboratory Lunatic

It was like a scene from a seventies science fiction horror film. Stella blinked rapidly, nearly reaching out to pinch her arm.

"Holy shit," Iris whispered next to her.

"What the flying fuck *is this?*" Stella hissed.

Iris covered her mouth with her palm.

The room was a laboratory in pristine condition. Clearly, this portion of the test site was thriving. Clean and shining glass beakers and test tubes lined polished silver counters in perfect rows. Blinding-white walls glowed under the fluorescent tubes lining the ceiling.

It was the hanging bodies along the back wall that made Stella's voice catch in her throat and her toes curl into her feet. Human. They *had* to be. Yet, it was hard to determine exactly what species *they* were.

One *thing* had its eyeballs removed from the sockets. Each of the white oculars, blood-red vessels snaking around their bulbous forms, stretched up over the head, still attached to the pulpy veins pulled taught from the pink, gaping, empty sockets. A tubular form of translucent flesh wrapped each vein, pulsing and morphing like an elongated amoeba. Its lips pulled thin in every direction, quivering as they opened and closed. All the teeth were gone. Glutinous pink gums remained, exposed and chomping at the air every time the mouth opened. Like it was trying to feed, as if it were *hungry*.

For what? What did something like this even eat?

As Stella examined it, her own body shivered with cold. Its fingers spread out, the skin between each stretched further than should be possible. Each finger elongated, the joints broken, the tendons stretched and pulled till they nearly snapped. Additional translucent flesh morphed with the original fingers, turning them into some sort of tentacles. Ruddy suction cups formed at the tips of the makeshift digits.

Bile crawled up Stella's throat as she looked at the legs, or the lack thereof. Gone. They were simply gone. The bulk of the body, the chest and torso, formed a heaving bulb of flesh. It ballooned and sank in a grotesque cycle, breathing life into whatever the thing was. It appeared to be *alive*. A composed human-octopus. That was the only way Stella could put into words what she was looking at. A dozen tentacles, ten from the fingers and two from the eyeballs.

Iris nudged Stella with her elbow. Stella startled, yanked her focus from the thing, then followed the direction that Iris was pointing.

There were multiple monstrosities. The *human-octopoid* was only the beginning. Iris pointed at another human creation. Whether it was male or female was impossible to determine.

A slice ran from its neck down to its groin. The skin peeled away from the centre of the body toward its arms, forming a pair of sheets. The sheets melded with similar peels of skin sliced and pulled from its arms. Similar flaying morphed the legs. Altogether, a single sheet of skin, as if sewn with invisible thread, formed a circle of flesh around the entire body, attaching the arms to the torso, the torso to the legs, and the legs together. No comprehension of the creature it was supposed to be came to Stella's mind.

Stella snatched her gaze away only to land her focus on the *being* next to it.

It was appendage-less. No arms. No legs. A head without ears. A smooth body, coiled, piling up on itself like a boa-constrictor. Its flesh pushed against its skin, overstuffed and about to burst. The outer shell of skin was thick with diamond shapes carved in an intricate pattern, caked blood rimming each one. Voluptuous breasts protruded from its chest, or where a chest would be if it were human, heaving with their fullness, hardened, pink nipples piercing the air. The worst part was the face. Its head, still looking human, but shaved clean of any hair, and ear-less, smooth like a crystal bulb, bobbed back and forth like it was trying to get its bearings. The face...with a wretched expression of horror mixed with loathing, pulled the lips into a grotesque grin, and made its eyes seethe.

Stella shook. She looked at the floor, took a deep breath, then swallowed back the half-digested dried toast and runny eggs she'd wolfed down at the diner only hours ago. What the *fuck* were they dealing with here? When had they stepped over the line from hunting human monsters to chasing a mad scientist making creatures far more fucked up than Frankenstein?

Iris clamped her hand on Stella's shoulder. "Did you hear that?" she whispered.

Stella listened. A clicking noise, like heels against a floor, echoed from the other side of the wall, right behind them.

She frantically looked around the room, wanting to find a space to hide. As much as her heart was telling her to flee from this lab of horror, her gut was gripping her like a guiding hand, telling her that if she walked away, then further innocent humans would fall victim to this madwoman's lunatic fantasies. Besides, fire blazed in her gut as her craving to inflict pain upon this killer scientist heightened.

She grabbed Iris' hand and pulled her to the right side of the room, toward a tall cabinet. She opened the double doors and stepped inside. Iris joined her. The cold of the steel wall seeped through her jacket, chilling her back as she latched the doors shut. Darkness dimmed the brightness of the sterile room. Her chest heaved as she steadied her breathing and quieted her mind. Iris fell silent beside her, the warmth of her thigh against her own.

They waited. Stella's heart pounded against her chest. Sweat broke out on her neck and back, despite the coolness of the cabinet. She wasn't sure if she was excited, or terrified, or both. She knew she was ready to pounce on her fresh prey. Yet, her instincts screamed that looking into the eyes of this killer, this lab rat turned crazed chemical mastermind, would ignite her desire, her already raging *need*, to slice, maim, and kill.

Chapter 19
Fish-Child

Stella huddled close to Iris, trying to steady and quiet her breathing. Her blood pumped hard through her veins and her heart thrummed against her chest. She couldn't wait to get a glimpse of the lunatic scientist removing eyeballs, peeling skin, and deforming humans into grotesque creatures.

Iris sighed and settled in beside her. The door slammed, sending an echo through the quiet of the sterilized laboratory. Stella pressed her face against the cold steel of the door, peering through a thin slit.

A harsh female voice barked instructions. "Lithen. Do a...as you are told, you *will* be fine. You thhow promi...ise."

Stella narrowed her one-eyed gaze on the two figures walking through the room. A tall, slender woman, wearing a shirt and pants that appeared to be made of some sort of thin, nearly transparent material. *Catrina Mortem. A.K.A. The Laboratory Lunatic.* Her stark, straight blonde hair fell down her back. A pair of plastic safety glasses perched atop her head, secured by a band that ran across the base of her skull. The heels of her tall boots clicked across the concrete floor.

Catrina hovered in front of the human-creature with the splayed, circular sheet of skin. "You see, thith ith what we can ath...achieve. You will be a matherpie...piece." Her tongue ran slowly along her upper lip, if you could call it a lip. It was a thin line, stretched and jagged. Thick red gloss smeared the deformed lip to smooth it, but resulted in a horrifying, blotchy effect.

"Her lip..." Iris whispered. "Her dad did that."

A child too young to be a part of this lunatic laboratory stood behind the woman, gawking at the humanoid creation. The child's skin had a scaly quality about it. Epidermis sheets pulled and melded, fusing its arms to its torso. The flesh between the child's fingers and toes pulled thin and fused, turning the hands and feet into some sort of flippers. Its bald head gleamed under the bright lighting. An orifice gaped openly where the child's genitals had once been, extinguishing all signs of gender.

A shiver trickled down Stella's back. The child, obviously the newest subject in this lunatic scientist's quest, no longer looked human. Iris breathed heavily next to her. Stella pressed her finger to her lips, encouraging Iris to quiet down. Iris nodded, then steadied her exhales.

The Laboratory Lunatic walked to the end of the lineup of her macabre masterpieces, pulling the child along by a chain attached by two clamps to what should be nipples but looked like reddened pimples ready to burst. The child-creature responded, its small, bare feet-flippers slapping along the floor.

A glitch shimmered in the room. The lights flickered. Stella blinked hard. The killer was slithering across the floor, a chain around her neck. Stella was pulling and yanking and yelling. She shuddered. *What's happening?*

Bright lights blazed then simmered. The crazed killer with the deformed lips pulled the chain. The child struggled to keep up.

They approached the far corner of the lab where a large rectangular glass tank sat against the wall, filled to the brim with bubbling, clear liquid. A replica of the one found here, in the same basement bunker that Dr. Mill Mortem had conducted his questionable experiments in, over a decade ago. *Was it the same tank? Had the mad scientist's daughter, now a crazed scientist herself, come all the way back here to use her father's equipment and to further his experiments? A family of killers.*

Catrina yanked the chain hard, pulling the clamps and stretching the child's already thin skin. Stumbling, the child's knees scraped against the rough floor. Whimpers escaped from the child's quivering lips. It curled its fused legs against its stomach, crying and shaking.

"Get up!" Catrina yanked the chain again. The fish-child jerked and flopped.

Iris pressed her hand against her mouth, muffling a cry and shaking her head. Stella glared at her, willing her to shut up. Breaking their cover now would ruin everything.

"We have to do something," Iris hissed as she shot a venomous stare at Stella.

"Not *yet.*" Stella pulled her mouth into a thin line.

Iris backed off, pressing her face harder into the door.

Circling the chain around her wrist, Catrina reeled the child in like a fresh catch. The child's body scraped along the coarse floor, ripping its scaly tender flesh, leaving streaks of green glazed ichor. Catrina attached a ring with a metal clamp around the child's neck and another around its lower fin-legs. Two chains, attached to each of the clamps, clanked, weaving around a long, cylindrical pulley above the tank as Catrina cranked a lever. The creature, now lying horizontally, raised up and over the tank. The chains halted. A loud bang echoed through the laboratory. The child hovered over the deep water.

"You will become what you were dethtined to be," she instructed in a husky voice.

Was she excited? Was this her ultimate fantasy? Did her father force her into a tank of water?

Iris stirred. "We can't let this child die."

"We can't *save* it. *Look* at it," Stella snapped.

Chains scraped and grated loudly as Catrina turned the pulley the other way, lowering the child toward the water.

The child's screams pierced the air, muffling as it plunged into the water. A burst of bubbles shot up from its mouth to the surface. Catrina slid a stepladder across the floor. A harsh scraping sound sliced through the room. Her boots clicked as she ascended to the top step and thrust her arm into the water, pushing the child's scaly chest down with her palm. The child's body trembled and shook violently as its flipper-arms flailed against the resistance of the water. Its entire body undulated as it swam in place. Its arms stretched out and the sheets of skin glided through the water. It almost looked like a human stingray. Gills carved strategically into the sides of its neck opened and closed. The child's underwater breathing eased into a smooth oscillation, its body billowing to the water's rhythm.

"You thee. Thith ith...is what you will be. My father taught me. I will thhow you the th...same." Catrina's voice escalated with excitement.

A sudden spasm shot through the child's body as its mouth opened and bloody bubbles polluted the water. Fighting to surface, the child spasmed again, thrusting its hand-fins upwards.

"No!" Catrina screamed. "You must let go."

Iris unlatched the cabinet doors. Stella grabbed her hard by the shoulder.

Iris yanked herself free from Stella's grip.

"*No*," Stella muttered.

Iris lunged for the woman, unsheathing her knife. She sliced across Catrina's back, tearing open the strange material and drawing a thin line of blood.

Catrina spun, jumped down from the ladder, and walloped Iris across the head.

Iris stumbled back. Her knife clanked across the floor.

Stella stood ready, boots planted, Beast Hunter drawn.

Catrina smirked, licking her lips. "Well, well. What do we have here? Two deliciouth creatureth...creaturesss, ready to morph."

Stella swung, slicing across the woman's shoulder, cutting open the plastic-like shirt, but barely slashing the skin. *Fucking Iris. This is a fucking disaster.*

Iris ran, screaming like a banshee, slicing low, cutting Catrina across the abdomen. The Laboratory Lunatic crumpled to the floor, clutching her stomach and laughing maniacally.

Stella grabbed a fistful of the woman's hair and forced her head into her own knee with loud crack. The woman hunched over, gripping her open wound with one hand and her face with the other.

Stella grabbed Iris and spun her around. "Cool it."

"We need to kill her."

"You want to give her a quick death? An easy way out?"

Gurgling and splashing halted their argument. The child struggled against the water, refusing to comply with its fishlike body, its mouth sucking in gulps of water as it tried to surface. Iris ran to the child. Catrina moaned, still crumpled on the floor. Stella strode to her prey.

Water gushed over the sides of the tank as Iris lifted the child, letting it hang over the side by the chains. She found the lever and lowered it to the ground. Its body flopped onto the floor, its mouth opening and closing, gulping in air.

With the handle of her knife, Stella smashed the side of Catrina's skull. The woman went limp, sprawling across the floor.

Chapter 20
Innocence

"She...he...it's alive," Iris' voice quivered as she bent over the fish-child twitching on the ground.

"*It.* My god. Listen to yourself!" Stella strode to Iris and the creature.

"It's a *life.* A *young child,* for fuck's sake." Iris narrowed her eyes, spitting her words.

"*Was.* Was a child. Look at *it. What kind of life* do you think this thing can have?" Stella tapped her boot against the floor.

Iris curled up next to the creature, cradling its face in her hands. Its mouth opened and closed, gasping for air. Its eyes filled with fear and despair.

Iris moved into a squat, slid her arms under the child's neck and fin-legs, lifting it as she stood. "We *need* to save it. We are supposed to be saving victims." She pushed past Stella, heading for the exit.

"Iris, wait. *Think* about what you are doing," Stella pleaded. A fire ignited through her. Her temples pulsed. What the *fuck* kind of life would this creature have? The psychological damage alone would be insane.

A whoosh of air swept over Stella. The Laboratory Lunatic lunged at Iris, knife in hand.

"Iris!" Stella sprinted toward them.

Iris spun.

The crazed scientist brought her hand down, piercing the blade straight through the child's heart. Blackened blood oozed from the wound, dripping over the scaly body and splashing over the floor.

"No!" Iris pulled the child closer and turned away, shielding the creature.

Stella plunged her knife into Catrina's back. She fell to her knees. Blood poured from the open gash, slipping down the transparent material of her shirt, and pooling on the floor.

Catrina hunched over on all fours and gasped for air. "You fucking bith...bitches! Tho...society doethn't appreciate my work. *You* don't either, throwing all thith away." She coughed, red saliva bubbling around her mouth as she frowned.

Pressure tightened around Stella's temples, her veins protruding from her neck. "You sick freak."

Catrina's sinister laugh sent a chill down Stella's back.

The woman spat bloody saliva onto the floor. "You do not thee the beauty. Just like all the otherth...wanting a demented definithon of perfe...perfection."

Iris screamed from a few feet away. The scaly body lay still in a black pool. Iris jumped up and ran at Catrina. Iris' boot connected with the woman's right cheek, crunching the bone and snapping the woman's head.

Catrina fell onto her side, cackling and spitting crimson foam. "You stupic bith...bitches."

Winding up for another kick, Iris swung her leg.

Stella pounced on her, pulling her from behind.

Iris spun around and faced Stella. "She *has to die.*"

Stella stroked Iris' arms with her palms. "She will," Stella whispered. "You will feel better if we do this slowly. Leave her with her own signature."

Inspecting the human creations lining the back wall, Iris pondered Stella's words. The room, now a scene of carnage, splattered in blood, infused with death, young innocent death, transuded a dark vibe. There was no turning back. There never had been.

Iris nodded. They walked toward the woman, hoisted her up by her arms, and dragged her over to an empty metal pole next to the tank.

Chapter 21
Slice and Sew

The Laboratory Lunatic hung by her arms, dripping with blood, her wrists secured by rings attached to a pole.

She smirked slyly. "You bith…bitches. You are both pathetic."

Something inside Stella snapped. The slow roiling of desire to inflict pain boiled over, surged up her body, and thrust a hot, metallic burst of bile up her throat. She clenched her jaw, swallowed the taste of the *need to kill,* and gripped her hunting knife so hard that her fingers swelled.

This was it. The reign of this mad bitch scientist would end now. A life for a life. And how many had this crazed *monster* taken?

Iris, standing beside her, trembled, her face reddened and dripping with sweat. "Bitch, you have *no idea* what we are."

Since she started this rampage, Stella knew the *desire* burning within, festering, turning her soul to rot. She'd seen it in the eyes of the killers she'd hunted, locked away, and even murdered ruthlessly. This was the first time she'd seen it in Iris' ice-blue pupils.

The killer licked her lips slowly, running her tongue along the thin, jagged scar with sadistic delight. "You try to take *my* creath...creation. My ultimate mathterpiethe. Thi...thisss is what you get." She flicked her head at the lifeless young creature.

Sweat drizzled down Stella's face, sticking wild strands of her dark hair to the sides of her cheeks. She narrowed her eyes and walked right up to the woman; her face a mere inch from hers. "It's your turn, *crazy bitch.*"

The woman spat. Bloody spittle stuck to Stella's nose, dripping down her face, pooling above her lip. She licked it, swallowed and smirked.

"You are sick." The woman grinned.

Iris sidled up next to Stella. "Now what?"

The shock and disgust when Stella desexed the Carnal Cougar had faded from Iris' ice-blue eyes. It seemed she was going to be a willing participant in the ensuing torture.

"Let's see what this maniac is hiding." Stella unsheathed her knife and approached their prey.

The steel punctured the plastic-like shirt below the woman's neck. Stella guided it expertly, slicing down the translucent material, splitting it open. Iris peeled away the sticky material. Iris gasped. Stella stood back and examined the remnants of Dr. Mill Mortem's experiments on his daughter. Scars, ragged, red, and inflamed, puckered and contorted the skin up the insides of her arms and along the sides of her torso, like half-sewn, infected seams.

"My father had a gloriouth...ious vision. I was to be a beautiful creature. Thome...something that no one had ever achieved." The crazed woman spoke matter-of-factly, as if her situation was usual. "They came in and took it all away before he could finith…ish." She swallowed. Her grotesque lips quivered. "Before he could complete me."

"So you thought it was OK to do this to a child?" Iris sprung forward, her face reddened.

"You don't understand. I thpent years with pthy…psychologists and doctors. They tried to fix me. They destroyed everything he had accomplithhed. I had to finish what he tht…started." The woman raised her head in defiance.

"We're wasting time," Stella said as she sliced her blade down the woman's right pant leg, then the left.

The clear plastic material crinkled away. Pinkish seams, bubbling with infection, ran down the woman's legs.

Stella loomed close until she could smell the fear-infused sweat trickling down the woman's face. "You will feel what you made them feel."

"You don't know how it felt."

"Then you can show me." Stella licked her lips, stepped back, then sliced the makeshift seam running down the woman's right arm clean open.

The woman wailed. "You fucking bitch!"

Stella strutted like a cat circling its prey. With her knife, she reopened the old wound running down the woman's left arm.

"What are you doing?" the woman screamed.

Bursts of excitement rippled through Stella, a jolt of heat sizzling her extremities.

Iris stood watching.

Would she become the partner Stella hoped she was? The partner she so desperately needed.

Iris exhaled, unsheathed her knife, then walked up to the woman. Sticking her blade into the top of the woman's thigh, she ran it down the inflamed line, giving the old wound fresh life. Blood oozed over the woman's misshapen flesh, dripping over her boot, and pooling on the floor.

Iris stood back, then smirked. Performing a similar procedure on the woman's right leg, flaying the flesh and exposing a wound from the past to the present moment. The woman howled like a wounded animal. Another bolt of excitement energized Stella's entire body, from her gut to her skull. Neurons sizzled in her brain. Sweat drizzled down her face and neck. She pictured Iris in her cotton panties, sprawled across a cheap motel bed.

Stella shook her head and focused.

"Now what?" Iris asked.

Stella clenched her jaw. She glanced at the dead child lying in its own ichor. "We make her look like that."

Iris stared at the child. Stella walked around the lab, rummaging through tools and chemicals. An instrument caught her attention. It was long, silver, thin, and had an eyelet. It looked like an oversized needle. Stella smirked and picked it up. She examined the glass bottles, finding one labelled nitrocellulose. She grabbed it—a syringe, a roll of wire, and a cutter.

"What's all that?" Iris asked.

"A taste of her own signature."

Iris followed Stella over to the hanging, bleeding woman.

As the sharp point of the needle pierced Catrina's skin, she cried out. "Thtop...stop. You dethroy hith work." Her voice seethed with anger. She writhed her body, but her movement was limited. There was no escape.

Stella injected several additional shots of the chemical until the skin started loosening, dripping away from the mad scientist's arm. At first, the woman cried out, but as the chemicals flushed through her veins, she could only muster a mere whimper.

Then, with her knife, Stella peeled away the flesh.

Catrina jolted. She screamed. "You deth...destroy...it...all..."

Stella stretched the sheet of flesh. The Laboratory Lunatic's eyes rolled back and her body went limp. Iris went to work injecting the skin plasticizer into Catrina's legs. Stella repeated the skin-peeling procedure along the woman's torso. Stella joined the two flaps of flesh. Catrina's body alternated between spasms and stillness as she grappled with consciousness.

"Hold this," she said.

Iris grabbed the epidermis and overlapped the edges, stretching them out. Stella cut a length of wire, threaded it through the metal needle, then positioned it at the base of the joined sheets. She pierced the sharp tip through.

Catrina bolted awake again with a spine-chilling scream.

Stella pulled the needle clean through the woman's flesh. Piercing a half inch from the first hole, she continued to weave the wire through. She stitched crudely, forming a seam until Catrina's arm attached to her torso.

Catrina's cries tempered to mere whimpers as she again drifted in and out of consciousness.

They stood back and examined the effect.

"It worked," Iris stated.

They repeated the process, fusing Catrina's left arm to her torso. After flaying and stretching the skin from the reopened seams down each leg, Stella pulled the flesh around both legs, wrapping them together, then fusing it. Catrina's legs conjoined like a single appendage. The woman's head repeatedly lulled forward, her eyes rolling back, as she teetered on the edge of blacking out.

Stella pierced the woman's leg with her knife, jolting her awake.

"Bbbiitchesss..." Drool pooled down the woman's chin.

Stella and Iris stood side by side, admiring their creation. Their killer masterpiece. Calm washed through Stella.

The woman's body shook, blood and sweat dripping over the fused, bloody and festering flesh. It was a crude creation, one that may have inflicted more pain and suffering than any of the other human creatures hanging from the wall had felt.

Stella unhooked the fish-woman and let her fall with a loud thump against the floor.

"Yyyoooou...biiitchesss..." a slightly decipherable raspy voice was all that the crazed killer could muster.

Iris pulled Catrina by the wrists and dragged her across the floor. Skin scraped concrete, ripping, tearing, and leaving viscous red streaks.

After securing the rings around the woman's neck and her legs, Stella cranked the pulley. The woman shrieked as her body shuddered, rising over the bubbling liquid. Iris stepped in and lowered their creation into the water. Her new body spasmed as she gurgled, trying to reach the air with her lips. Iris cranked until it was impossible for the woman to surface. Water flew, splashing over the sides of the tank and splattering onto the floor.

Stella took Iris' hand in hers and led her back from the water where they stood in silence, watching the lunatic scientist, the tormented woman, the human monster, their creation, spasm and fight until she drowned in the very tank that her father had taught her to swim in.

Chapter 22
Release Me

The two-star rating of the motel room couldn't be accurate. Despite Stella's love for a run-down shithole, she'd barely give this place a single star. Maybe even a half. An odour of mothballs and sweat assaulted them when they pushed the door open, holding their breath that it wouldn't fall off its hinges.

The humanoid creations loomed in her mind. A lot of dead bodies had floated through her life. Never had she seen anything so deformed, grotesque, *inhuman*. After the spree of purges they'd been on, exhaustion should take over. Instead, she kept replaying the torture they'd inflicted upon The Laboratory Lunatic. Skin ripping as she pulled it away from the killer's body echoed through her ears, a horror soundtrack soothing like the sounds of the ocean. Catrina's crazed howling vibrated through the walls of her mind, reassuring her that her job was well done. If only the victims could have seen and heard.

Part of her wished she could have put them out of their misery, but she knew Iris couldn't stomach a moment more in the sterile laboratory.

The door to the mini-fridge slammed shut, intruding on Stella's reverie. Iris walked toward her, a bottle of bourbon in one hand, two plastic cups in the other. She'd read Stella's mind. Every cell in her body vibrated on high. Hot tingles of lust tickled her arms and legs. What she wouldn't give for a good fuck. An earth-shaking orgasm would release her from replaying her kill on repeat, clinging to the high and yearning for another taste of blood. But reaching a sexual climax was out of the question. Iris wasn't going anywhere, and it had been increasingl y difficult for her to make herself cum. She had several cuts now, on her abdomen, and up her inner thigh. The freshest one was deep. Requiring an increasing amount of pain and blood each time, the last experience frightened her.

Iris handed her one of the plastic cups, full to the brim with sweet amber liquid, then plunked down on the bed. She gulped back half the bourbon in her own cup. Her shoulders shuddered. She looked more shaken than Stella had ever seen her.

Iris' voice sounded small and lost. "That child…" A tear trickled down her face to the corner of her trembling mouth.

Stella gulped indulgently from her cup as she sat down next to Iris. Heat swelled up her thigh as it pressed against Iris. "It's not our fault. If we didn't go there…there would be others. We stopped it."

"Sure." Iris huffed. She drank back the rest of the liquor in her cup.

Stella had never seen her like this or drinking this much this fast.

"It shouldn't have died." Iris poured another full cup.

"No. But it's not *our* fault." Stella brushed Iris' hair from her face. "It was damaged…beyond hope."

Iris looked at the ground.

"We fucking killed her. It's over. No more innocent victims," Stella said.

Iris chugged the second pour in its entirety, then dropped the cup. She turned and hovered close to Stella. Cinnamon enticed Stella. Cherry lips called to her. Sweat trickled down the curve of her back.

Iris leaned forward and pressed her lips to Stella's. Stella's body quivered. Iris pressed her lips harder against Stella's. The plastic cup slipped from Stella's hand, falling to the floor. A waft of alcohol rose as bourbon soaked the crusty carpet. Springs creaked as Stella's back pushed against the cheap mattress. Iris mounted her and planted spicy kisses down her neck. A trail of sweet saliva lingered on Stella's hot skin.

Iris shoved Stella's shirt up over her head, then explored Stella's body with her tongue. She halted and sat up.

"What the..." Iris whispered hoarsely.

Dammit. The scars. "I...*need* it."

"What?" Confusion and fear poured from Iris' eyes.

"To cum. I need pain. And blood." Stella's face flushed.

Iris ran her hand over the scars etched crudely across Stella's abdomen. "The broken mirror in the bathroom," she whispered. "It wasn't an accident."

"It was. I got so frustrated." Stella gritted her teeth. "You've seen me, the way I get when I'm killing one of those fuckers. I need them to feel the way their victims felt."

"I get it. You saw me today." Iris' finger lingered on the deepest scar. The newest one, still half-formed.

Stella flinched and sighed. "After, it's like I have to release all that pent-up, fucked-up energy. I need sex. Or some form of it. But...I can't *release*. Not without pain. And blood." Stella swallowed and clenched her jaw.

Iris' lips pulled into a thin line. She reached over and cupped Stella's face with her hands, then leaned in and kissed her hard and passionately. Stella gave in. Completely exposed, no part of her wanted to hold back.

Iris kissed her until Stella was sticky with her own sweat. She pushed Stella back hard onto the bed, then hungrily ran her tongue down Stella's body, lingering over the most severe of her self-inflicted wounds.

Iris pulled Stella's pants off, threw them on the floor, and parted Stella's legs. She paused at the sight of the half-healed cuts along Stella's inner thigh. She pushed her tongue against Stella's clitoris, hard and intentionally. Stella's body responded. The room whirled. Dizziness and heat consumed her. Several times she came close to climaxing, but each time she yearned for pain and to taste blood. The craving wouldn't subside, no matter how hard she concentrated on Iris' tongue against her, inside of her.

Iris stopped, walked over to the table across the room, retrieved the knife she'd used on their last kill, then returned to the bed. She flipped Stella over onto all fours, then licked Stella from anus to pussy.

Hot moisture oozed from her as Iris inserted her tongue into her vulvar slit. Mini-eruptions built again. Saliva pooled at the back of her throat, yearning for a taste of copper.

Her skin sizzled, craving a slice of pain. Iris pressed the edge of her knife against Stella's plump ass cheek, just hard enough to pierce the outer skin.

Stella jolted at the prick. Fluids seeped from her pussy. Iris licked them away, then pressed her tongue against Stella's clit again. She slid the knife along Stella's flesh, just enough to inflict a stinging pain and a trickle of blood.

Stella reached back, slid her finger along the wound, then brought it to her mouth and sucked. Iris worked Stella's clitoris in circles, increasing the pressure. Fluids gushed from her as her body shook. Every victim floating through her mind vanished, their whispers silenced. Her mind cleared. A sense of calm after the storm flushed through body.

She fell against the bed, face first, spent and satisfied.

Chapter 23
Too Pure for a Purge

It was quiet in the half-star motel room. Despite how thin the walls were, silence cloaked the entire building. Stella sat at the round table beside the mini-fridge, drinking bourbon straight from the bottle. After going down on Iris, they used their fingers to bring each other to a second, powerful climax. Iris sliced a fifth cut into Stella's abdomen to make her reach orgasm. It wasn't as deep as the one she'd inflicted upon herself, but it worked. It didn't take long for Stella to pass out as Iris lay close next to her.

When she woke, she heard Iris retching in the bathroom. It may have been the shots of bourbon, full and fast. Although Iris normally held her liquor well, tonight she'd thrown back drink after drink at a frightening pace. Stella suspected the slow slaughter they'd inflicted upon the crazy scientist, *Catrina,* might have pushed Iris over the edge.

Stella had expected her new purging partner to handle the torture and killing better than herself. After all, Iris had been chasing serial killers much longer than she had. Now, she wondered if Iris had been on the good side too long to stomach the extreme level of butchering she'd been inflicting on their prey. The peeling and sewing of skin on The Laboratory

Lunatic had been a team effort. It was the first time Iris had been completely involved. Maybe Iris wasn't *like her*.

A soft snort from across the room brought Stella back into the moment. After upchucking every bit of the cheap, overcooked steak she'd consumed at Rob's Roadhouse, Iris crawled under the covers and curled into a ball. Stella stroked her white-blonde hair until her breathing deepened and she settled.

When Iris joined her on this insane purge, becoming a killer of killers, tunnel vision took Stella down a clear path. She hadn't thought twice about it. Hell, Iris had even admitted that she'd callously murdered the suspect in her last case. That she'd *chosen* to go after him, and ended up leaving him in a worse state than he'd left his victims in.

Now, after Iris' emotional reaction as she watched the creature child die in her arms, after she'd joined in on the slow slicing and sewing of skin, and leaving the killer scientist in an inhuman state, Stella suspected that the strong and confident Iris was broken.

The silence thickened. Iris snored softly. Stella took another long pull of the bourbon and tried to quiet her mind. She knew she had to continue to purge the worst killers on the earth, with or without Iris. She only hoped she hadn't caused irreparable damage to the one person in her life.

LOVE

Chapter 24
Atomic Liquor

The 70s Rock-Ola jukebox clicked as a record slid into place and the needle dropped. A glint of light reflected off the shiny black disc as it spun. "Peddlers of Death," a song from an older *Black Label Society* album, was a prime find in this run-down joint. Sorrowful piano chords ran through the room. A soft, yet metal-edged voice beckoned Stella to take a hand. She wondered if she could save Iris, if she could save herself, or if they were both destined to drown in a bloodbath. As she turned, a blast of electric guitar cut through her heart, pulling her from the depths of despair, and pumping fresh energy into her veins.

The heels of her boots stuck to the floor as Stella walked to the back corner of the joint. A red glow outlined Iris' silhouette. Her partner in crime sat on a high stool, hunched over a rectangular table. They hit the road late. Wanting to put some distance between them and the lunatic scientist, they drove all day. After shooting west to cross into Nevada, they meandered south on the less travelled roads. They hadn't spoken a word about the human-creature they'd molded, or about how Iris had facilitated a blood-soaked sexual release for Stella.

Stella hoisted herself up onto the stool across from Iris. She took a long pull of the cheapest bourbon she'd ever consumed.

The liquor burned like acid as it slid down her throat. Her arms and legs instantly numbed in response. *Atomic Liquor,* tucked away in a forgotten corner of Fremont Street, didn't offer Woodford Reserve, but it was the perfect place to blend in and take a break.

From the moment Stella had first laid eyes on her, Iris had never looked her age. Until now. The neon lighting amplified the veins riddling her bloodshot eyes and doubled the size of the swollen bags under them. Stella wondered how much longer they could go on like this. A thick silence hung between them. Stella couldn't take it. She reached over and placed her hand on top of Iris' clammy hand. Iris shot back the rest of her drink, grimacing at the burn, then set the glass down. The song turned back to weaving melodic piano and voice, weighing down her soul again and reminding her of the burden of pain.

Stella stroked Iris' hand with her thumb. "Look...I..." The words wouldn't form.

Iris sighed, her shoulders heaved. "Let's just...*not.*" Desperation tainted her raspy voice.

Stella clenched her jaw and nodded. Iris was right. They couldn't, *shouldn't* talk about any of it. They both knew what had happened. Both of them had changed. The *need* to torture and kill infested them both now. Sex had morphed into a pain-gorged, blood-drenched, post-kill release for both of them. And they had broken their promise *not* to fuck each other again.

"Another?" She nodded at Iris' empty glass.

"Why the hell not?" Iris chuckled. It was the first time she'd mustered up anything resembling a smile since they'd left the Teiko test site. "Let's drown our sorrows in this cheap-as-fuck bourbon, crash in that sleazy motel next door, then restart when the sun comes up over this dusty, lonely desert." Iris squeezed Stella's hand.

The change in tone in Iris' voice provided the first ray of hope in days.

"Sounds perfect," Stella said.

Iris returned to flipping through and examining the stack of newspapers she'd gathered at gas stations and run-down convenience stores as they'd driven through Utah and across Nevada. Grabbing their empty glasses, Stella slid off the stool.

Iris gasped. The tabloid shook in her hands. Her shoulders trembled. "It can't be," she whispered.

"What?" Stella popped herself back up onto the stool.

Iris slid the paper across the table. *Decomposed, Dismembered Girl Corpse Found.*

Beside the headline was a photo of the body of what must have been a young girl. The body had one arm. A long black dress, caked in dirt, covered the half-decomposed figure. Several jagged lines ripped open the skin above her upper lip.

"Dolly Dorah." Iris' eyes glazed over as she looked past Stella, her lips quivering.

Stella knew this look all too well. "An old case?"

Iris licked her lips. "Yeah. I need another drink. Now."

"On it." Stella jumped down again.

As she grabbed the glasses, Iris clasped her by the arm. "I don't care how fucked up all this is making me. I need to chase this one."

"No. *We* need to."

Chapter 25
Henricas

The door opened slowly, creaking on metal hinges, echoes piercing the silence. Concrete walls, painted in red splotches, closed in, suffocating them in icy darkness. The room smelled wet with a tinge of something *infected*. A steady bleep-bleep vibrated through the darkness. Silhouettes of figures appeared along the back wall. It was too dim to be sure, but Stella could swear they were children.

Stella's jaw clenched hard, grinding her molars against each other. Beads of sweat dotted her forehead. Iris grabbed her by the hand and squeezed. As her eyes adjusted, she no longer doubted what she saw.

A row of *human dolls*, the only way she could think to describe them, along the back wall. Each of them, somehow standing, yet lifeless, cloaked in sleeveless black dresses, concealing the horrors inflicted upon their small bodies. Each of them with a single arm, the left one missing. Six pairs of obsidian eyes stared vacantly at them. Whitened skin, like porcelain, stretched smoothly over their faces. Their lips, an unnatural red, slightly parted, each with a precisely carved two-inch incision chiseled up from the point where the left side of the top lip turned upward.

Replacements for a disfigured and deceased daughter. Dolly Dorah, forty-five years old, no longer able to conceive, still mourned the loss of her only child, Henrica. The girl was born *perfect,* according to Dolly. Three days after her sixth birthday, a car hit her as she rode her bike on the quiet street in front of her home. The driver, disoriented by that extra glass of wine and daily double dose of Valium she'd become accustomed to, didn't even notice when the hefty steel bumper of her Cadillac knocked the child right off her bicycle. It wasn't until the front tire pinned Henrica's left arm to the ground that she felt the bump and pumped on the brakes. The car rolled right over the appendage before coming to a full stop, detaching it from the girl's body. This and the two-inch scar ripped jaggedly above the left side of her lip were the only visible remnants of the accident. The rest of her injuries were internal. After three days in the hospital, she died of internal bleeding.

Dolly snapped. She devoted her life to recreating her dear, deformed Henrica.

The six Henrica replicas swayed slightly as they stared, their black eyes sending a chill through Stella. Cold sweat drizzled down her arms and back.

The bleeping sound heightened, then eased into a steady blip-blip, coming from the left side of the space, where an operating room table pressed against the wall. A small, quivering body spread across the table.

Iris grabbed Stella by the arm and nodded at the body.

The moment she saw the photo of the young girl in the news article, Iris knew it was another version of Henrica. She described the extensive profile she'd built of Dolly Dorah fourteen years ago. All of it still vibrant in her memory, like it had happened yesterday. Dolly had slipped through the fingers of the FBI and vanished. Iris had never let it go. The images still burned so brightly in her mind, she described every detail over several double bourbons, stronger than gasoline. The specifics were so meticulous, Stella could swear she was looking right into Iris' mind.

Stella and Iris stayed up all night examining maps and combing through searches at a twenty-four-hour Internet cafe. The girl's dismembered body was tucked in the bushes of the summit at Angels Point. Images of the abandoned Linda Vista Hospital, only two hours from Angels Point, painted a picture eerily similar to the operating room that Dolly had fashioned in her basement to create her six Henrica replicas back in 1987.

As they approached the fresh victim, an icy claw scraped up Stella's insides. Her gut told her that this was *all kinds* of *off*. When they reached the table, Iris gasped. Her hand shot to her mouth, her fingers shaking.

A young girl lay with her eyes closed, her body quivering in a slight, steady tremor. Long needles pierced the girl's arms and neck, attaching clear tubes to her skin. The tubes wove their way to a steadily blipping machine beside the bed, lit up with an eerie blue glow, lines stretching across its monitor in strange shapes. A thin hospital gown stuck to the girl's body with bloody patches soaked through. Her chest rose and fell in a slow and steady cycle.

Iris reached out and grabbed the bottom of the gown, then slowly lifted it away from the girl's body. Stella wasn't sure she wanted to see what was underneath. There was no stopping Iris.

Iris stood paralyzed, staring at the replica of a dead child, tears streaming down her face.

"It's her." Iris' voice was a hoarse whisper. She turned and faced Stella.

Stella closed her eyes and tried to numb herself from the sound of Iris crying. She pictured a person who could do something like this. It wasn't a person at all. It wasn't *human*. The lunatic, the psycho, the monster that did this needed to pay. Heat soared through Stella's veins. Her mind sizzled with electric thoughts of thrusting her knife over and over into the flesh of this human monster, cutting off her arms, hacking into her legs, making her into a freakshow worse than any Henrica replica she'd created. Hatred and anger rushed through her. She opened her eyes. As she looked at Iris, her heart seized.

"We never got her. This...this is *my* fault." Tears streamed down Iris' face.

"No. It isn't. We can end this now," Stella said.

Stella startled at a prick in the back of her neck. Iris went limp beside her, collapsing to the ground. The room went black.

Chapter 26
Sacrifice

Blackness turned to an invasive bright light. Stella blinked rapidly. The back of her skull thrummed worse than any bourbon hangover she'd ever had. She tried to lift her arm to wipe the sweat from her face and pull the sticky strands of hair from her eyes, but it wouldn't move.

"What the…" Her throat was so dry it stung.

The Henrica replicas along the far wall came into focus. Her wrists, rubbed raw from the binds securing them to the arms of a metal chair, stung like hell. Pain sliced across her ankles when she tried to move her feet.

Shaking her head back and forth, sweat and hair fell away from her eyes. The young girl, still on the operating table, now completely naked, whimpered and shivered. A balled-up cloth gagged her. Her upper lip stretched thin, clips securing the skin on both sides.

Iris. Stella scanned the room frantically. Iris, tied to a chair, sweating profusely from every pore, her entire body shuddering, looked straight at her. Fury seeped from Iris' dilated pupils.

Holy fuck.

Her arm. It was gone.

Cut clean off. Clotted blood caked the blackened flesh around the gaping hole. *What the hell had happened?*

Iris lifted her trembling fingers away from the arm of the chair, revealing the obsidian gem of her beloved necklace. A loud creak. Iris pressed her fingers over the gem, hiding the makeshift weapon.

The slow clicking of boots crept up behind Stella. She clenched her jaw. Her stomach turned in knots. Closing her eyes, she rested her chin on her chest, pretending to remain unconscious. The clicking heightened and then eased. Stella dared to open one eye halfway. A woman with short, scattered raven hair and cloaked in a long, dark sleeveless dress walked away from her. *Dolly Dorah.* It had to be.

Dolly loomed, her face inches from Iris'. "Agent Quesnel. *Iris.* After all this time. I thought I would never see you again."

Iris pressed her lips into a thin line. Her body convulsed then eased back into a steady tremor.

Dolly stepped back. "We will have so much fun." She ran her fingers over a series of large meat cleavers mounted on the wall next to the girl. After selecting one with a hefty rectangular blade and a cherry wood handle, she held it up. "But first, I must finish making Henrica perfect."

Delusional Dolly. That's what they should have called her. Did she actually think that this half-dead girl was her daughter? Of course, she did. Stella knew better than to question the deranged fantasy of a psychotic killer.

Dolly set the cleaver down on the table above the girl's head and picked up a tool, a sort of mini jigsaw, and clicked it on. The saw whirred to life. Barely pressing the edge of the jagged power blade over the girl's upper lip, she guided the buzzing tool upwards. Blood sprayed. Muffled cries pierced the air. Dolly hummed while she worked. Stella quickly recognized the melody as the child's nursery rhyme, *Rock-a-bye Baby.*

Iris leaned over, gripped the obsidian between her teeth and sawed the sharpened point back and forth against the tie around her wrist. Dolly hummed louder to overcome the drone of the saw. Suddenly, the wire broke and fell to the ground. Iris' nostrils flared. She slid the gem into her back pocket, then leaned her body over her knees and worked at the bindings around her ankles.

Iris stood slowly. Her entire body convulsed. Sweat slicked her face and stuck her white-blonde hair to her skin. She steadied herself, shaking her still attached limbs until they responded to her command. Silently tip-toeing over to Stella, she nearly stumbled several times. Once Stella's right wrist was free, Iris turned toward the killer and the victim.

"Wait..." Stella whispered.

Iris either didn't hear her, or she ignored her completely.

Stella worked quickly at releasing her other wrist and her ankles. The buzzing of the power tool halted. Dolly hummed louder. Teetering from side to side, struggling to maintain her balance, Iris approached the crazed woman from behind. Dolly gripped the cleaver and raised her arm right above the girl's left shoulder.

Iris' entire body, slick with sweat, shook as she stood, staring at Dolly. Suddenly, she stilled. She lunged, thrust her body upwards with the strength of her right leg, and came down chopping Dolly's arm with a forearm blow, just in time. Bones crunched. The cleaver clanked to the floor. Dolly came up, arm bent, elbow connecting with Iris' nose. More bone crunched. Blood poured from Iris' nostrils. Dolly spun and stuck her fingers right into Iris' open stump.

Iris screamed. She fell to her knees.

Dolly bent down toward the fallen cleaver.

Stella ran for the wall of cleavers, grabbing a butcher knife with a curved, elongated blade. She double gripped the walnut hilt.

Dolly swung the blade over Iris' right shoulder. The high-quality steel sliced clean through Iris' flesh and ligaments, right between the humerus and the shoulder blade. The free limb landed with a sickening squish in a pool of blood. Iris lost her balance and fell forward face first.

Stella lunged, raising the butcher knife over her head.

Iris, armless, blood pouring from the fresh, gaping hole, face down on the floor, spasmed and twitched.

Just as Stella reached Dolly, Dolly turned. Stella swung. The blade sliced into Dolly right below her rib cage. Dolly gasped as she dropped the cleaver and gripped her side. She crumpled to her knees, blood oozing from the gash, coating Dolly's fingers.

Stella rushed to Iris' side and turned her over onto her back. A shard of rusty metal protruded from Iris' right eye.

"No..." Stella could barely speak.

Blood oozed from Iris' wounded eye. She opened the other one, staring at Stella with a single arctic-ice pupil. Her lips moved. Stella leaned over to hear what she was whispering.

"Save the girl..." Her eyelid closed.

A wave of tears pushed against Stella's eyes. She shook her head, clenched her jaw hard, stood, then walked over to Dolly, gripping the knife with whitened knuckles.

Chapter 27
Dismembered Dorah

Rage broiled through Stella. Her veins pumped with hot lava anger.

Iris, propped up against the wall, beside the row of Henricas, stared at her with a single glassy, lifeless eye. This was for her. This—*all of what was about to happen*—was for Iris.

Dolly Dorah, with her arms and legs stretched out in a cross formation, her neck secured against the wall, blinked lethargically. Stripped naked so that Stella could see exactly where she was aiming. Conscious enough to know what was going on, to feel pain, to fight for her life.

Gripping the massive butcher knife with both hands, knuckles white and skin coated in blood, Stella bit her lower lip and raised the blade up over her head. With slow, determined steps, she walked up to the killer. She swung the cleaver down hard, right into Dolly's left arm. High grade steel cut clean through. The arm swung, the wrist tied tight. Stella swung again, slicing through the bind. The arm fell to the ground, landing in a pool of Dorah's juices with a loud splat. Droplets of blood sprayed Dorah's naked body and Stella's arms and face.

Stella smirked.

Dorah's eyelids fluttered as her eyes rolled back.

Stella smacked her hard across the face. "You *don't* want to miss this."

After stepping back a few steps to provide room to reposition the cleaver over her head once again, Stella stepped forward and swung the blade clean through Dorah's right arm. The armless woman cried out. The meaty appendage hit the ground with a squishy sound, landing next to the other arm.

Stella strode over to the six Henricas. As she moved past each one, she spoke to Dorah.

"You sick, psychotic, poor excuse for a mother. Who lets their child play near danger?"

"I...no...I didn't know..." Red saliva dribbled down Dorah's chin.

"A real mother would never inflict pain on a child. Not even a child that wasn't her own." Halfway down the line of Henricas, Stella shot a glare at Dolly.

"I *neeeeed*...them..." Dorah's upper lip cracked open, sprouting fresh blood.

"You *need* to feel what you made them feel." Stella stopped at the last Henrica. She moved toward Iris. Poor, armless, dead Iris. How did she let this *happen*?

A fresh wave of anger hotter than the flames of hell rose through her. With long strides, she returned to Dorah. It was time to finish this off.

Positioning the cleaver to the right, she aimed the blade at Dolly's left leg, just above the knee, and swung with all her might. The blade sank into Dorah's flesh. Tendons tore and bones cracked. Flesh ripped open. She hacked several times until Dorah's lower leg detached and fell.

"Nooo…" Dorah screamed, scarlet mucus bubbling from her nostrils.

Sweat dripped down Stella's face. She licked her lips, then repositioned the cleaver. After four hacks just beneath Dorah's right knee, it came free. Four appendages piled in the pool of blood beneath Dorah.

Dorah's eyes rolled back. Her head lulled forward, her chin squishing against her sweat-slick and blood-coated chest.

Heat flushed Stella's body. "This is *all* for Iris."

She positioned the cleaver again and swung it straight for Dorah's jugular.

Chapter 28
Thirteenth Angel

A neon-white cross lit up the night sky, bathing them in pure light. Stella cradled the girl in her arms as she looked up at the peak of Our Lady Queen of Angels Cathedral. The white bathed the entire building, a beacon of purification in Stella's life drowning in blood. She kneeled and carefully settled the girl on the ground next to the daunting wooden door.

She'd pressed her fingertips into the porcelain necks of each of the six Henricas. None of them breathed. They were all dead. Dolly Dorah had claimed a dozen young girls in total. The six found in her basement in 1987. Six in the abandoned hospital. *How many others had there been?*

The girl stirred. The bandage across her upper lip pulled as she tried to speak. Her eyelids fluttered. Her head lulled, and her body stilled.

After dismembering Dorah, Stella remained in the abandoned hospital. Using discarded supplies, she'd crudely stitched and bandaged the jagged cut across the girl's lip. She hoped it would heal without too much scarring. The girl had been through enough. It was a miracle the girl still had both her arms. Images of Iris attacking Dorah and dislodging the meat cleaver from her killer clutch invaded Stella's mind.

What was Iris thinking? She couldn't let another young victim die at the hands of the killer that she had failed to stop. It wasn't Iris' fault. Yet, Stella knew the feeling all too well. She put the blame on herself for losing victims many times. As if it weren't a sadistic killer that slit the neck of an innocent being. As if it were her hand guiding the blade. A heavy ball of guilt welled in her gut at this very moment. The thought that Iris' death was her fault blazed in her mind.

This time...she could have done more.

The look in Iris' arctic-ice eyes as she released Stella's wrist from its wiry bind, as she turned away from Stella, as she faced the killer that had slipped through her fingers fourteen years ago, stuck in Stella's mind. It haunted her soul. She'd never forget it.

Iris' dying words whispered through the cold air...*save her.*

The girl lay still on the ground. Her steady breathing reassured Stella that she'd done what Iris had asked. Stella curled over her knees and kissed the girl's forehead. She was the thirteenth angel, and Iris had saved her.

Her hand trembled as she grabbed the massive knocker and pounded it against the door. At the sound of footsteps, she bolted to the side of the building.

As she walked away, the chill of the night stung her tear-stained cheeks. A cinnamon scent wafted through her nose as memories of Iris flooded her thoughts. Fire-red hair. Ivory skin. She slipped her hand into the inside pocket of her jacket and retrieved the obsidian gem, the only thing she had left of her fellow killer. She wrapped her fingers around the stone. The sharpened point pricked her fingertip. Droplets of blood burst from the puncture. She sucked on the tip of her finger. The metallic trace on her tongue brought a fresh wave of memories. Iris, in her cotton panties, slicing her knife into Stella's flesh. Heat sparked through Stella's limbs.

Amping up her pace, she spotted her car two blocks down. She didn't know what lay ahead. It might be a lonely road. The desire to kill burned inside her.

She slid into the driver's seat, closed the door, and turned over the engine. The silence was too much. The cassette clicked as she pushed the play button. A thrumming drum and guitar assaulted the entire space of the car, jolting her. Her skull wrenched as she cringed and faced the barrage of horror flashing through her mind.

Armless Iris face down in her own blood. Dolly Dorah screeching obscenities as her limbs fell. The heavy walnut handle of the insanely large butcher's knife, slick with scarlet internal juices, slippery yet soothing in her hands. The squelch of the blade sinking into flesh, over and over.

As the chorus of the song, "Thirteen Years of Grief," unfolded, the singer's rough-as-rock voice wove around her soul, reminding her how motherfucking tough she thought she was, accusing her of being nothing more than an ignorant punk. A dynamite guitar riff reverberated with high energy. The song had a firecracker essence, like Stella.

Would she suffer the thirteen years of grief he spoke of? One for each of the young angels taken under Dorah's torturous care? Iris died believing the girls had lost their limbs and had their faces sawed because she couldn't stop a crazed killer. Even the one that she saved. What would her future be with a jagged scar marking her, reminding her every waking moment of her life of the psychological terror she'd suffered under a maniac mother's hand? A glaring symbol of how the world had failed her when it was supposed to protect her.

Stella slipped her flask from the glove-box and doused the ball of sick at the base of her throat with an ample swig. She rested her head against the seat, relishing the burn and the numbing. Capping the flask, she tossed it onto the passenger seat as she revved the engine and peeled away from the cathedral.

Chapter 29
Stella's Scream

The purple Pontiac Sunbird blazed down the windy road, leaving a wake of dust. A dynamite riff blasted through the speakers, reverberating through the car. "All for You" by *Black Label Society*. Stella checked the rearview mirror, revealing the deserted road behind. Empty. Like her soul. She glimpsed the short locks of her rust-red hair whipping recklessly in the wind from the open window.

She wasn't Stella anymore. Or perhaps she was more *Stella* than she'd ever been.

Exploring the void of the empty desert on remote roads at night and sleeping off mickeys of bourbon in cheap motels during the day, she'd been on a three-day adventure through southern California, alone. Trekking over the back roads through the Anza-Borrego desert and meandering around the Salton Sea, she was on her way to feed her soul with a dose of metal like no other. Grasping for a sense of purpose, it might be the only way to jolt herself back onto some sort of track. Other than gas stations and motels, the only stop she'd made was to slip a postcard into a mailbox in the quiet town of Salton City.

The gravelly voice seeping from the speakers told her it was *all for you.*

She slid her hand into the inside pocket of her leather jacket and pulled out Iris' gem. The obsidian glimmered as she set it down on the dashboard. Cold rushed through her gut. She clenched her jaw.

As she hacked Dorah to pieces, dismembering her limb by limb, had it all been for Iris? The only *you* she'd known since leaving her life behind and embracing her transformation into a full-fledged killer. Her metallic-laced, lustful craving for blood and the thrill that shot through her thinking of the obscene chopping and the weight of the butcher knife proved she needed this. With or without Iris. Yet, she knew her execution of a mourning mother had resulted from her feelings for Iris. She doubted she would have saved that girl if it hadn't been Iris' dying wish.

Zakk's voice dissolved her reverie. The dark road snaked around the black hills ahead. Stars clustered in bright swirls, beacons in the midnight sky. The words of loss, no hope, and slain emotions caused a surge of heat through her body. The song burned energy through the car, its essence like the firecracker FBI agent Stella invited into a savage rampage. It was *all for her.* Stella couldn't turn back now. If she did, then Iris' life would be inconsequential in a world drowning in evil. Iris meant more than that. To her. And to every victim she'd ever saved. Including the one she'd died for.

The road stretched out long and dark. Stella tightened her jaw and pressed her boot hard against the gas pedal. The engine revved. The car surged forward, careening down the road, into the darkness.

Tilting her head back, Stella opened her mouth and screamed. She screamed for Iris. She screamed for every innocent victim she'd failed to save. She screamed for her own soul.

Her scream simmered. Her eyes opened. A sharp bend in the road appeared. She cranked the wheel to the right. The wheels spun. Dust flew. The rear of the car fishtailed. She gained control just in time. The road opened up again, shooting straight into the cold, dark void of the empty desert.

Chapter 30
Pavilion

A deep, hypnotic guitar riff thrust through the entire amphitheatre, reaching down inside of Stella and gripping her soul. "Love Reign Down" was one of her favorite songs. As she wove through the back of the crowd, the pace of the electric strums amped up, and the vibe in the open space intensified. She hovered at the point where the crowd thickened. She wanted to be close enough to feel the energy seething from the veins of her favourite metal singer, but she wanted some distance from the other sweat-soaked bodies.

As the rough voice sang to her of love reigning down, she wondered if her postcard made it into the hands of the amber-eyed man that wouldn't leave her thoughts. Mesmerized by the performance, only the third song in, seeing the frontman take the stage once again was even better than last time. His boots rooted to the stage, his bulging biceps pulsed as he shredded the strings of his purple and black bullseye Gibson Les Paul, and his long, sandy-blond hair fell in a thick curtain over his face.

As she took a long pull on the double bourbon in the cheap plastic cup plastered with the *Talking Stick Resort* logo, she exhaled deeply and drank in the moment. The outdoor theatre in the heart of Phoenix was massive and well set up. Despite the number of metal lovers at the show, the space was ample, creating pockets of less packed areas. It was a relief for her to have a bit of space. Usually, she'd be at the lip of the stage, fighting off gem-doused sluts to keep her centre spot. Tonight, she simply wanted a good dose of raw metal, some double bourbons straight up, and a bed. Maybe she'd even splurge on accommodation with a high enough star rating to offer good bourbon and a hot bubble bath.

It was New Year's Eve. Most were making resolutions for fresh starts. She hadn't the faintest clue what her next move would be.

The guitar went into Mach speed, blasting electric bullets through the open space. The metal-edged voice of the singer cut into her heart, telling her of what she wanted and what she needed. Closing her eyes, she tried to clear her mind of carnage, corpses, and death.

A hand touched her shoulder. Prepared to tell whoever the fuck was bothering her to go to hell, she spun on her heel and stared into the dark eyes she'd been thinking of only moments ago. Her breath caught.

"Bryce." Her voice was thick with shock and bourbon.

Bryce, the early thirties, amber-eyed forensic chemist from her long-left-behind past, stood here, right now, in front of her. He smiled as he reached out his hand and cupped her cheek with his palm.

"Detective." He smiled as he handed her a fresh bourbon. "Got your postcard."

"It's just Stella," she said as she took the drink. "Thank you."

He nodded.

"You knew I'd be here?" It was a stupid question.

"A postcard of the Talking Stick Resort Amphitheatre, where Black Label Society is playing their last show before leaving for another continent...uh, yeah. I knew you'd be here." He chuckled. "I thought you'd never ask...."

She tried to speak, but didn't know what to say. Just as the last chorus blasted from the stage, repeating words of love reigning down over and over, Bryce turned Stella to face the band and wrapped his arms around her, leaning her back against his warm chest.

Chapter 31
Rust

Stella dropped the needle. Sonorous acoustic strumming filled the room. The shiny black record spun. She fell into a state of hypnosis. Still amazed they'd found an old turntable at Roy's Records on the outskirts of town, she relished in the sound of Zakk's grit-laced angelic voice as it gripped her soul. The merch booth at the Talking Stick Amphitheatre was bursting full of Black Label Society shirts, albums, buttons, and patches. She had her heart set on the *Stronger Than Death* LP the moment she spotted it. The cracked cassette had lost its lustre on the long drive, from the belly of the prairies to the edge of the barren desert. Some sort of nostalgia had also taken over her, birthing a desire to remember the days when she was on a virtuous path.

The song opened up, and a soulful riff edged with grit ripped through the room. She held the LP cover, staring into the black eyes of the skull outlined with red curved spikes, reminiscent her Beast Hunter's blood-drenched blade.

Bryce approached from behind and pressed his tender lips to the back of her neck. As Stella succumbed to his touch—gentle, loving, *good*—she closed her eyes. He turned her to face him. His breath was hot and sweet as he pressed his lips to hers.

Guiding her to the bed, with his lips still glued to hers, he pushed her down hard against the luxurious mattress. A five-star treat, compliments of Bryce. Jaw clenched, she shivered with excitement. He knew she liked it rough. The first time, the only time, he'd made her climax, she'd forced herself upon him at the peak of grief.

His amber eyes devoured her. He pulled his shirt off as he leaned in over her. The heat from his body heightened the fire already raging inside her. He ripped her shirt open and tore it off. The tip of his tongue ran up her abdomen, lingered over her breast, then toyed with her hardened nipple. As he licked up her neck and found her lips, he paused, his eyes looking past hers, into her, finding her soul. She shuddered.

Her heart seized. Could she do this? Every part of her screamed to let him in. Aching for his hard cock to slide right up in her, yet terrified of the emotional repercussions. This was a brand-new emotional state. Not even Iris had this impact. Iris was the ultimate sexual release, daring to slice her open to help her cum. She was a desperate solution when Stella screamed for help.

This was something entirely different. As was the kill that started the series of slaughters. What would happen if she let go?

Bryce pulled away, his lips lingering for a moment longer against hers. After slipping her pants off and tossing them aside, he migrated down her body, pausing as he touched the rough scars tainting her flesh. The wounds that highlighted her desperation every time she looked in the mirror and begged for release after a bloody kill. From the anger sizzling on her skin and forcing her to slice flesh. From the life that wasn't a life. He pressed tender kisses onto the self-inflicted wounds without hesitation. Without asking questions. He moved down, toward her pleasure spot. He clamped his teeth around her lace panties and pulled until they ripped to shreds, completely exposing her. Taking a deep whiff, his nostrils flared. He licked slowly, with intention, from the base to the tip of her pussy.

Her body quivered as she arched her back and sighed. It was no longer a choice. She had to let go. Eyes closed, lips parted, noises of pleasure escaping from within, her mind wandered into a new place. A shiny new place with golden lights. Was there a new way for her? Would he understand her darkest desires? Her inability to orgasm until she sliced her flesh open. Her addiction to licking the sanguine fluids from the blade after a slow slaughter. The jolt of electricity and extreme excitement every time she killed.

Bryce slipped his tongue out and lingered upward until they were face to face. As she stared into the rich amber of his eyes, she violently shivered with raw heat. Their eyes locked. He kicked his pants off. As his rock-hard cock slid in, she completely succumbed. No longer in control of her mind and body, tingles ignited in every nerve ending as he thrust deep and slow, finding a hidden erotic zone.

She closed her eyes and drank him in—his sweet odour, his skin sticking to hers, the tingle of ecstasy building with each thrust. As she lost all inhibitions, she went deeper into this new glittering place. The golden lights blazed brighter the closer she came to climax. No blood. No pain. Just pure pleasure.

The guitar wailed, winding to a climax, then easing. The rough yet soothing voice of the singer declaring that rust tainted shiny things.

So close to the ultimate release, the halcyon lights suddenly dimmed, and the place became dark. Until all she saw was a black wall, peeling with strips of rust. Blood oozed from the open gashes. The peels curled as they fell to the ground, piling on top of each other, building a rust tower. The blood now poured out in streams.

Bryce. She focused, feeling him inside of her. The pleasure, the simmering ecstasy, the hope—it all returned. She let go again quickly, rebuilding to a climax. Just as she was about to receive that ultimate spark, the black wall reappeared, opening like a massive cavern. A rushing river of blood burst through, massive waves of roiling red, washing away Bryce.

She was in the middle of it, surrounded by a daunting scarlet pool. Her hand raised from the surface, blood trickling down the tip of the blade, over her fingers, binding her palm to the handle...forcing it where it belonged.

About Author

Julie Hiner spent endless hours during her childhood lost in the pages of books. The only thing that took precedence over a book was her Walkman. To this day, Julie is a hardcore 80s rocker at heart.

In a previous life, Julie worked as a computer scientist, specializing in network simulation. On a break between contracts, she published an inspirational work of non-fiction, her own story of facing fear and anxiety on a bicycle in the European mountains.

Julie now writes psychological horror/suspense and extreme horror heavily infused with hard rock and metal. Under her Killers and Demons imprint, she has published an *80s metal murder* detective series, a 90s nostalgic serial killer novella, and a death metal meets demon possession novella. She has also co-curated a horror anthology, and had several horror short stories published in anthologies. Her most recent work, Fear of the Deep, was published by Torrid Waters of Crystal Lake Publishing. You can find her at KillersAndDemons.com serving up toxic cocktails of metal and murder.

Acknowledgments

I have spent a lot of time writing alone in my office with a cup of coffee and my fuzzy blanket, however, writing this book was not a solo effort. There are many amazing people in my life that support me every time I embark on a new project. Thank you to every single one of you from the bottom of my little demon heart for all the warm hugs, cold beers, words of encouragement, sweaty nights of dancing, and head bangs.

Thank you to the AWCS (Alexandra Writers' Centre Society). They have supported me since the beginning of my writing journey with courses, networking events, and huge opportunities to be a presenter and a teacher. They have embraced my movement into more extreme horror and have provided a space for me to make an impact in this genre.

Thank you to Bradley Somer. Your course on theme completely re-aligned and focused this crazy novella into something with heart and focus.

Thank you to Cody Anstey for once again coordinating a soundtrack to bring my book to life. Thank you to Toryin Schädlich for sharing his amazing talent as a lead guitarist on all my soundtrack projects. Thank you to Duncan McCartney,

Grant Potter, and Lili Garbar for sharing their talent to make the soundtrack for this book happen.

Thank you to Andrea, my angel friend that was sent to me. Thank you for the fancy coffee time, the lunch dates, the stream of miniature animal videos, and the plethora of fuzzy and glitter coated gifts.

Thank you to Taija Morgan for taking on my first work of pure extreme horror like it was the most delicious dessert she's ever tasted. Her commentary on my manuscript pushes me to work harder while keeping me utterly entertained.

Thank you to James Hiner for all of the inspiration and support, and for showing me that 'yes I can' when I'm not sure. Right when I need it, he's always there to take me on a forest walk, for a plate of nachos and cold beer, or to sit through another true crime documentary.

Also By

Detective Mahoney Series:

Final Track – Book 1

Acid Track – Book 2

Back Track – Book 3

Devil's Track – Book 4

Thrash Track – Book 5

Torture Track – Book 6

Dead End Track – M.E. Blackwood Story

Novellas:

Owen's Terrarium

Metal Demon

Fear of the Deep (Published by Torrid Waters of Crystal Lake)

Anthologies:

The Omens Call – Edited by Hiner and Willcocks

Short Stories:

Ice Metal Queen, Solstice in Purgatory, The Seventh Terrace□

Attic Puppet, Terrors From The Toy Box, Phobica Books□

Candy Lady, October Blood, Hawke Haus Books□

Hallowed Killer, Pulp Harvest, Blood Rites Horror□

Corpse Forest, The Other Side, Devil's Rock Publishing□

Tuny, Terrace VI: Forbidden Fruit, The Seventh Terrace□

Hand of Doom, Hand of Doom: A Literary Tribute to Black Sabbath◻

If you enjoyed *Stella's Scream,* please consider leaving a review on Goodreads, Bookbub, or your retailer of choice. A review is worth a lot to an author.

Come visit @ KillersAndDemons.com